I0554056

Talons of the Eagle

by

Joy Brighton

Talons of the Eagle

Cover Art by *Jennifer Greeff*

The Wild Rose Press, Inc.
PO Box 708
Adams Basin, NY 14410-0708
Visit us at www.thewildrosepress.com

Publishing History
First Edition, 2021
Trade Paperback ISBN 978-1-5092-3736-4
Digital ISBN 978-1-5092-3737-1

Published in the United States of America

"I've missed you," I whispered to my ghost.

Missed you too. He touched my face, drawing his hand down the side of my cheek in such a simple, loving gesture. Tears gathered in my eyes.

Don't cry, Forrest.

I finally had the courage to open my eyes and watched him for a long minute. "It's all I've done."

His lips pressed together in a brief, heartfelt frown, but then he kissed me.

"Show me," I whispered in his ear. "I need to understand. Please, Josh. What should I do next?"

His thoughts entwined with mine, and I ran with him up a pine-covered hill. The Magician waited for us near the top. We followed him until we reached a ridge I'd never hiked before, and I looked out over the valley. The casino glowed in the distance. Its garish lights glared against the growing darkness of the desert.

"Is this where the Magician brought you before?"

Yes.

"What does he want?"

For the last of his tools to be returned to him.

"But you brought him the spear and even the eagle feathers. Wasn't that enough to stop Patterson?"

We didn't need to stop him. We needed to help him.

"How?"

We needed to help him move on.

Now I was more confused than ever. I had more questions, but Josh shook his head and tucked my hand under his arm. He hugged me to him, and I could feel his warmth, his breath, his heart against mine.

"Can I stay with you?"

You can't.

"It's too hard to be without you."

Norah will help. Listen to her.

"Should I go through with what she says? Should I undo time?"

Dedication

For indigenous people around the world who struggle to secure their rightful place.

CHAPTER 1

I stared down to the creek sparkling at the bottom of the gorge and gulped in a breath of frozen air. Man. It had to be a thousand feet to the rocky floor of Walnut Canyon. My brain fuzzed over, and I clutched at the heavy rope to keep from falling over the precipice.

Drawing in more air through my nose, I swallowed the prickly-pear lump gouging my throat. The oxygen helped clear my head, and I squinted at the far side of the red rock canyon. The late spring storm had cleared early this morning, and the bright blue sky contrasted with the snow-layered pines. The wind was calm. Perfect for climbing.

Manny tugged on the belay rope attached to his truck's tow bar one more time and attached the carabiner to my safety harness. "Ready, Josh?"

Adrenaline had my heart pounding like a jackhammer. I shifted my weight from foot to foot, and my boots squeaked in the snow. I pulled my wool hat over my ears and nodded, not enough spit left in my mouth to form words.

"Got the gloves?" George asked. My cousin and guardian said the words calmly, but there were deep lines in his wrinkled forehead and around his mouth. After I nodded and patted my back pocket, he walked over to double-check my equipment one more time.

Manny made final adjustments to his own harness,

1

jangling as he walked over to me.

He pounded me on the back. "Take it slow." His tone all business. "The nest is a few feet to the right of where we're dropping you. Just swing over when you reach that outcropping." Manny pointed about forty feet down the side of the sheer cliff to a miniscule ledge.

Didn't look like the flimsy shelf would support a squirrel, much less an almost-eighteen-year-old guy.

With my tether wound around his arm, Manny braced his feet to support my weight. He nodded. "Harness looks good. All carabiners locked."

No choice. "On belay," I replied.

"Belay is on."

"Descending." Still slightly dizzy and, I admit, shit-ass scared, I turned to face the men, leaned backwards, and stepped into oblivion.

I rappelled the first five feet and then dropped another ten. I checked my location, braced my legs against the wall, and slowly walked my way down the side of the cliff to my destination. I kept my gaze on the granite wall a few feet in front of me. If I looked down, man, I'd puke for sure.

I grabbed the rough perch. Icy snow froze my numb fingers to the cliff edge, but I dug for a toehold and swung my body closer to the nest. My rope held, and I steadied myself on the slippery rock.

A stone dislodged under my foot and tumbled into the ravine. Several seconds later, it hit bottom. Fear roared back through me, echoing in my brain and lancing down my spine. I held on, closed my eyes, and slowly counted to ten in the ancient language my mother taught me.

"Doing okay, Josh?" Manny called from above.

I glanced up at my mentor, squinting into the bright sunlight. The deep blue sky was clear, and the canyon's red rocks glistened with frost. At this altitude, the air was so fresh I could smell the piñon pines up on the mesa.

"Almost there," I called. I clenched my jaw and repositioned my aching hands. I'd spotted the narrow ledge, and grunted while I climbed down the last ten feet to the rocky outcropping. In spite of the cold, sweat beaded on my forehead and trickled into my left eye. I hissed at the fierce sting.

The ledge to my right was littered with an enormous collection of sticks and twigs, but was still wide enough for me to stand on. Three downy chicks about the size of scruffy pigeons huddled in one corner of the nest.

I tugged on the line. "Slack," I shouted.

"Slack." Manny gave me a little working room. "Don't touch the nest," he called down. His words echoed across the canyon.

I grimaced. *Like I didn't already know that?* Leaning into the rock wall to balance myself, I pulled the never-worn work gloves from my back pocket and used my teeth to yank them on one at a time.

At my feet, the spiky-feathered chicks squawked at my movements, raising their beaks in hopes of food.

"There are three," I hollered.

"Great."

I watched the golden eagle hatchlings huddle together for a few isn't-that-cute moments. Their soft gray down kept the babies warm even on this cold morning.

Mother eagle had returned from her hunt and

circled above me, pissed. I closed my eyes for a moment and thanked her for her sacrifice. She shrieked, then shrieked again. Her frantic mother's cry bounced between the canyon walls. I don't think she understood. Would any mother? After all, I was going to steal her baby.

"Which one?" I called.

"Take the big guy."

"But will the others survive?"

"They'll have a much better chance if that bruiser isn't in the nest," George said. "The oldest one will do the best with us." He lowered another long rope with a large, decorated bag attached to it.

I grabbed the ceremonial leather bag and quickly scooped up the hatchling. He squawked, and struggled to free himself.

I held him close for a moment. He stopped wiggling, and I felt his strong heart beating. "I know, fella. But you will have a wonderful life, and be much honored by the tribe. It is fitting." I spoke to him in my ancient native language to make sure he understood.

He called to his mother, and she gave a long, sad cry in return.

My heart squeezed, and I fought back the sting in my eyes that wasn't from sweat. I knew what it was to be an orphan, to be torn from family and raised by others for a purpose. "Don't worry. I'll take good care of you. You and me, we'll do just fine."

Feet first, I nestled the chick in the bottom of the bag. When I had cinched the bag tightly closed, George pulled the hatchling up the cliff. Manny tightened my rope so I could climb back to the top of the mesa.

****

4

"Josh just called," I yelled down the stairs into the small woo-woo tourist shop my gran and mother ran in Jerome.

Mom's face appeared at the bottom of the steps, and she smiled up at me. "Is he coming home soon, Forrest?"

"Tonight."

Across the shop I heard a muffled comment from Gran. Mom turned toward her and laughed.

I came down three steps and peeked under the banister. "What'd Gran say?"

"Your gran said, 'Good. Now maybe she'll stop mooning around the house.'"

I straightened my shoulders and raised my chin. "I hardly ever moon."

"Of course not, dear. But you have missed Josh."

"Well, sure. He's been gone all spring break." I tromped down the rest of the stairs, but thought better of giving them my scathing eye roll. Besides, being pissy was no way to get what I wanted. And right now I wanted to drive my jeep, Tilley, down to Verde. "Can I go meet him?"

Mom nodded and stepped back to study the display of Tibetan bowls I helped her unpack that morning. "Go soon," she added. "I don't want you driving Tilley on that road after dark."

I gave her a thanks-for-being-so-cool kiss on the cheek and ran back upstairs to grab my stuff. Finally Josh was home, and I had so much to tell him.

****

I parked Tilley in front of the Sorcerer's Trading Post a few minutes before six. The store windows were dark, and the town of Verde was closed up tight. An old, rusted-out pickup clunked down the road, trailed by a cloud of noxious fumes, and then the town of Verde was quiet.

An almost full moon rose in the eastern sky, big and round and golden. I watched it sneak above the mountain peak in the distance and thread its way through the newly budded-out cottonwood trees. Josh called again a few minutes ago. He, Manny, and George had stopped in Flag for dinner, but would be home soon.

I closed my eyes and thought about kissing Josh until my heart beat faster. A warm, delicious flush raced over me. I had missed his touch, his kisses. I had missed the way he looked at me with his gorgeous amber eyes. A tingle rippled down my back.

I know. It had only been two weeks. Not even. Twelve and a half days. I let out a sigh. Maybe Gran was right. I had been mooning.

But soon we'd get our college acceptances. Soon we'd graduate and go off to college together. Soon we'd have lots of time alone. Totally alone. I zipped my track jacket, snuggled down in the driver's seat, and smiled to myself.

Truck lights reflected off my mirror, appearing at the end of the road. I scooted up to check them out. The lights flashed, and I squealed with happiness. I jumped out of Tilley and waited for George's four-wheeler to stop in the alley.

Josh jumped out and grabbed me around the waist. He picked me up and twirled me around until we were both dizzy and laughing.

"I missed you, Josh." I kissed him hard. When he kissed me back, our tongues touched, making me even more breathless.

Shivers rolled down my spine. Wonderful shivers. When he set me down, I wrapped my arms around his neck and smiled up at him. I loved that he was so tall.

"I missed you, too," he whispered in my ear. "Come see what I found."

Manny and George were unloading suitcases, pretending not to watch our reunion, and giving us a moment. Josh led me over to the truck and pulled a large chicken wire cage out of the back seat.

Something moved inside, but I couldn't see it clearly in the dark alley. It made a raspy noise and moved again, bouncing against the side of the cage.

"Hush, fella. It's okay. This is Forrest," Josh said in a soothing tone.

"What is it?" I asked, moving my face closer.

"He." Josh flipped on a miniature flashlight. "It's an eagle. A golden eagle chick."

I glanced up at Josh, then down at the bird, confused. "Why do you have an eagle? Aren't they protected? Is he hurt? Is that why you have him? He's pretty small—and kinda beat up? Did you rescue him?"

Manny chuckled and turned toward George. "Does she always ask so many questions?"

"Pretty much." George grabbed two duffel bags from the hatch and disappeared through the back door of the Trading Post.

"My mother encourages questions," I said to the cop with more than a little huff.

Manny shot me a conciliatory grin and lugged a sloshing ice chest inside.

Carrying the cage, Josh swung his other arm around my shoulder, and we walked into the kitchen. "I need to get this guy into his new home. He's been cooped up in a cage most of the day."

I followed Josh through their small kitchen and out into the tiny back area usually used for storage. When he flipped on a light, I noticed a large enclosure that hadn't been there before.

"When'd you build this?"

"We finished it last week, before we left. Manny helped." Josh opened the door to the room-sized cage, set down the small carrier and reached inside to pick up the scruffy bird.

"Looks like he's been through a war," I said from outside the coop.

"He's not even fledged. These are his baby feathers."

On a raised platform in the corner, sticks and brush made a shallow-bordered nest with leaves and soft feathers lining the middle. Josh gently placed the bird in the nest and pointed to a switch on the far wall. "Can you flip that on?"

When I did, a heat lamp began to glow above the nest.

"This will keep him warm at night."

I gave a long sigh and waited for an explanation.

Josh smiled and glanced up at me. He rose, brushed off his knees and locked the door of the enclosure. "No more questions?" He reached over and put his arm around my waist to draw me closer.

I gave a quick shrug. "You'll explain everything when you're ready. I imagine this has something to do with the Magician. Did your ghost ask you to do this?"

"Ah. Another question."

I poked him in the ribs with my elbow. "Well, I'm

curious."

"Well, I'm starving. Let's eat. Then I'll tell you about it."

I had to laugh. The guy had his priorities.

****

I finished off my second ham, cheese, roast beef, turkey and pickle sandwich while Forrest quietly stirred the hot tea I made for her.

Manny left a few minutes ago, anxious, I think, to go see Grady. George said good night and closed the door to his room, leaving us alone.

I rinsed my plate off, put it beside the sink, and sat down next to Forrest. I let out a long sigh, but then straightened my shoulders and met her curious gaze. I wasn't sure she was going to understand all the implications of what I had to tell her. I took her hand and stroked her strong fingers for a moment, hoping the right words would come to me.

Sometimes it's difficult to explain the ancient customs of my people. Forrest was always willing to learn, but I had a feeling this tradition wasn't going to be easy for her to accept. It certainly wasn't for me. I swallowed hard. Where should I start?

I rubbed my hand over my face and then back through my hair.

"This is upsetting you," Forrest said before I even opened my mouth.

I frowned. I hadn't felt her read my thoughts, but maybe she was getting better at slipping in and out of my head.

"I don't need to read your thoughts, silly. I can see by your tells you're nervous as a guilty perp in front of a judge."

This time I really laughed. She pushed my shoulder, and I kissed her on the cheek. "Not easy having a girlfriend who's training to be a cop. Grady's been teaching you more about interview skills?"

"Joshua Kwail, really. You totally aren't that hard to read." She straightened and gave me a brilliant smile. "Fess up. What's going on with the poor itty-bitty birdie?"

"I'm going to raise it."

She opened her mouth to question me, but I put up my palms. "Don't worry. We have permission to take it. Not that Manny thinks the tribe should need permission to continue with a thousand-year-old tradition, but George says it's easier that way."

"Where'd you get it?"

"Out of his nest."

"But golden eagles always nest on cliffs." Her eyes went very wide and very, very blue. "You climbed down a cliff to get the poor little thing?"

"Yeah. But it wasn't too hard. Manny had me roped in. The snow made the rocks a little slippery, but other than that…"

"You climbed down a cliff in a snowstorm?"

"No, after. The next day. Honest, Forrest. It was no big deal. Perfectly safe. I climb higher cliffs all the time." My bravado was easier to pull off now I was back on solid ground again.

She twisted her mouth, and her I'm-thinking-really-hard expression flashed across her face. "Okay. But I still don't understand why you would want to do such an idiotic thing. Is it a Yavapai tradition?"

"Hopi. Remember, my mom was full Hopi. From Moencopi."

"So Hopi boys are supposed to go out and catch an eagle. Some sort of coming of age ceremony?"

"Kinda. Not everyone does it. Just…"

"Just a shaman. Or future shaman?"

I nodded. Now for the hard part. My stomach felt a little sick. I licked my lips and looked away. I was pretty damn sure how Forrest would react to the next part of my story.

She smoothed her long hair back from her face and studied me closely. "So is the bird your familiar, like in Harry Potter? I assume you're going to raise him. Are you going to teach him to hunt? Or is he part of the magic from the Magician?"

"He is part of the magic, but it's not like he will live with me for a long time. There will be a ceremony and he will…"

I dropped my gaze to stare at my hands, realizing they were clutched together so tightly they ached. I couldn't say it. Couldn't tell her I would have to watch the beautiful bird die. His feathers would be sacred only after he'd been sent to the Fifth world.

"Feathers?"

I glanced up, surprised she'd caught my thought. Her eyes, so blue a moment ago, turned a dark green. Her lips thinned to an almost invisible line.

"Josh. You wouldn't." She stood, almost knocking over the chair. "You'd kill him for his f—." Her breath hitched. "His feathers?"

"It's part of the tradition." I still questioned the value of custom myself.

"Tradition? Are you crazy?"

I stood and reached for her.

"Don't," she hissed and dodged my grasp, her

palms facing out.

"You don't understand," I shouted.

"Got that right." With tears damp on her cheeks, she grabbed her coat and slammed the door on the way out.

I kicked the chair in frustration. Damn. I knew she wouldn't understand.

I ran after her, but she was fast. She'd already started Tilley before I could reach the jeep. "Forrest. Wait." I said through her closed window. "I know this is weird, but before you leave like this, I want you to do something for me."

She turned her hot, angry gaze on me, and I almost stepped back, but I straightened my spine and stood my ground. "Read me."

"What?"

"You heard me, dammit. I dare you. Read me. Look inside my thoughts and try to understand."

She stared over my shoulder for an extremely long minute, still breathing hard, but when I touched her hand, she didn't pull away. "Please. It's important that you understand."

Forrest turned off the engine and sucked in a couple more deep breaths. I could read tells, too, and knew from her body language she was trying to control her anger. Man, she was pissed. I waited, barely breathing myself, until we both calmed down.

"Look at me," I whispered.

She looked up, her cheeks still wet. I brushed my thumb down the side of her face and took her hand softly in mine. She turned to me, and I prepared for her inspection. I had to be fully open to her, ready to accept her. I squared my shoulders and dropped my shield.

"It's okay, Josh," she whispered.

"No, Forrest. I want you to understand."

"I already do."

"I don't get it. I didn't feel you do anything."

"I don't need to." She squeezed my hand. "I'm sorry. I reacted to this whole thing without thinking about who you are. What you're preparing for."

Now my eyes began to sting, and I turned away.

She crawled out the jeep and into my arms. "I love you, Josh. As much as I hate the thought of killing any creature, I know you would never do something that didn't have a…" She stared at the dark, star-filled sky for a moment, like she was searching for the right word. "A vital purpose. It won't be easy for me, but if the little eagle is part of your tradition, then I'll try to accept it, because I accept who you are."

She laid her head on my chest. I held her and tears flowed down my cheeks. We were both a leaky mess. My heart felt so huge I struggled to breathe. No one in all the years since my mother died had anyone accepted me so fully. I pulled her closer and kissed her cheek. "I love you."

She stepped back a fraction. "I love you too." But the sorrow in her eyes reflected the real truth in my heart. Taking my eagle's life would be the hardest thing I would ever have to do.

Forrest cuddled under my arm. "What did you name the poor little guy?"

CHAPTER 2

Josh asked me not to tell anyone about his bird. I got it. For sure, not everyone would understand the ancient, totally-not-politically-correct ways of his people, but I had to talk to my mom, and I hoped he'd understand.

"Aren't you upset?" I asked her when I finished telling her. We were sitting upstairs in our living room. Gran was out doing one of her Tarot readings, and we had an evening alone.

Mom glanced over at me with a quiet smile. "You mean because when I was young, I was so invested in protecting creatures like the spotted owl?"

"Yeah. I needed to tell you about the eagle, but I wasn't sure what your reaction would be."

She smirked. "I can imagine what yours was."

I leaned my head back against the cushions and stared at the ceiling. "Got that right, at least at first."

With a short chuckle, Mom pulled the soft blue shawl from the back of the couch, draped it around her shoulders and snuggled back into the pillows. She pushed her short hair her brow and seemed to be thinking hard about what to say next. After a long moment, she glanced at me. "I've always taught you to respect living things."

I nodded, but fiddled with the cuff on my sweater.

"I gave up meat years ago." She rubbed her

14

forehead with her thumb. "The Hopi people, and the Yavapai for that matter, have lived in this region centuries longer than we have. They live with nature in a way that's almost impossible for us to understand, much less accomplish. Josh is an important link in the heritage of his people. If raising this eagle is part of his tradition…their tradition, then we have to show respect and support him."

My chest ached and my eyes overflowed. I crawled next to her, and she put an arm over my shoulder.

"I don't know how he'll do it." I whispered.

"What?"

I leaned my head in. "Not fall in love with him."

She drew me closer. "Maybe loving the bird is part of the process."

****

"Josh."

My room was dark and cold. I rolled over and struggled to open my eyes. "Huh? What?"

George nudged my shoulder again, and I sat up. The light in the kitchen glowed softly around his shadowy frame. "Your bird's squawking."

I glanced at my clock. The dial flashed 3:30 a.m., and I groaned. "I just fed him at one."

"Well, he's hungry again."

I listened more carefully and heard the bird's plaintive screeches. I set my feet on the icy floor and rubbed my eyes. "Guess the alarm clock in his nest didn't work." I stepped into my shoes and grabbed my jacket.

"Guess not." George shuffled back toward his room.

I grabbed a baggie of raw hamburger from the

fridge and dragged my sleepy carcass out to the pen. Dumb bird had dumped over his water bowl again and was soaking wet. I wrapped him in an old towel and sat down on a stool in the corner of his pen.

He was shivering with cold, so I pulled him close to me until he warmed up. I held the meat in my fingers the way Manny had showed me, and the little guy took it from my hand. "There you go," I said softly. He took another bite. "Not too fast, now."

I smoothed back his sprig-like feathers and patted his back. After another few bites, he settled in on my chest and stopped flapping his stubby wings. He gazed up and seemed to be studying me. I spoke to him in the old language.

"You will be my partner in this world.
You will be my messenger to the next.
You are the special one.
My messenger.
The one the tribe needs to bring peace to our land."

He tucked his beak down under his wing and let out a long sigh. His breathing changed, and he slept. I scooted us closer to the heat lamp. Guess I was staying here for the night.

****

"You look like hell," Forrest said when I saw her second period the next day.

"Up all night with the bird. Again." I shoved myself into the too-small classroom chair and cradled my head on my hands on the top of built-in desk.

"Need some help?"

"George is going to man the night shift tonight. He knows I need some rest. I could hardly stay awake in

16

AP Bio, and it's my favorite class."

"Rough night, Mr. Kwail?" Miss Abernathy stood, arms crossed, at the front of the room. When most of the class turned to stare, my ears tingled with embarrassment.

I sat up straight and gave her a weak smile. "I'll be okay."

"Were you up late studying for my quiz?"

I groaned to myself. Shit. What quiz? I was screwed.

By lunch I was so tired I couldn't even eat. Forrest let me sleep on the grass in the shade for the whole hour. Somehow I stayed awake through the afternoon and met her in the senior parking lot before track. I felt like a zombie. Probably walked like one too.

"You look beat," she said, inspecting me closely.

I gave her a halfhearted shrug and grabbed my track bag from the back seat of her pink polka-dot jeep. "I'll make it."

She crossed her arms and put on her don't-mess-with-me face. "You should go home."

"Can't. Coach needs me to work with the freshman sprinters today. He wants them to improve on their starts from the blocks."

"The track meet isn't until next Saturday."

I nodded and kept walking.

"Josh," she called from behind me. "You should let other people help you."

"I'll get some rest tonight."

"No. Now. I'll work with the guys."

I stopped for a moment.

She perched her fists on her hips and shook her head. "Darn bird is nothing but trouble."

I turned to face her and smiled down at her stern expression. Then I laughed.

"What so funny?" She looked insulted, like I was teasing her for saying something stupid.

"Trouble."

"So?"

I grabbed her by the arms and grinned. "I've been trying to figure out a name for the eagle for days now. Nothing fit."

"You're going to name him Trouble?"

"Well, he'll get some sort of official sacred name from the tribe, but that's what I'll call him."

When she laughed with me, I felt energized. More awake than I'd been in a several days. "Come on." I took her hand. "Help me with the freshmen. Then we can both go home early."

She smiled up at me, her face all sunshine and love. My heart turned over and my ears heated. She was so beautiful. I nudged her firmly against the side of the jeep and stepped between her legs, kissing her hard, and winding one hand into her long, soft hair. She moaned against me and wound her arms tightly around my neck. Her warmth and softness always turned my brain to mush.

Then my stomach growled and she giggled.

"You got anything to eat?"

****

I drove Tilley down to Verde early on Saturday morning, shielding my eyes from the glare of the rising sun through my windshield. I had the whole day to hang with Josh and, better yet, Mom said I could stay overnight at the Trading Post.

That was new. She and George must have a plan.

Or maybe they just figured Trouble would keep Josh and me too busy for anything else.

I found Josh in the kitchen looking rested. With a welcoming grin, he handed me a cup of coffee, shoved another piece of toast in the toaster, and punched down the lever.

"George took the night shift again?" I bit into the buttered toast he passed me, crunched, and licked the apricot jam off my lip.

"Yeah, but Trouble only woke up once in the night. Then he slept until sunrise."

"That's great. He's getting bigger. Bet his stomach can hold more food now."

"And he's stopped knocking over his water bowl all the time. We wired it up on the side of the pen so now he doesn't get wet and need to be dried off."

While I chewed on my toast, I noticed the stack of books on the back of the kitchen table. *Birds, Raptors and Eagles* was the top one. I pointed the toast at the book. "Been reading up?"

Josh nodded. "George ordered them from the library in Prescott. He hasn't raised an eagle since he was my age. Said he needed to brush up." Josh picked up the oversized book and thumbed through to a marked page. "Here's Trouble."

"Wow. That's a golden eagle?"

"He'll triple in size in the next couple of months, fill out his feathers. He should be ready to fledge in a few more weeks."

I had to chuckle.

"What?" He looked up from the page.

"You sound like a proud papa."

I could see the blush burn on his cheeks, so I

squeezed his hand. "Sorry. Didn't mean to tease."

"No, it's okay. He's family now, and I'm proud of him. We're supposed to bond. He'll be my messenger, so he needs to be strong and beautiful."

****

After breakfast, I offered to help Josh unload T-shirts and restock the shelves in the Trading Post. Once he and I finished his chores, we'd have time to go for a ride, and I wanted to drive up to Oak Creek Canyon. It would be warm today, and the winter rains would have the river running high. George had offered to bird-sit, and even packed us a picnic lunch.

I glanced down at Josh. "Manny didn't tell you, did he?"

Josh looked up from the cardboard box he was cutting open. "Something about Trouble?"

"No, about him and Grady."

Josh shrugged and handed me another stack of shirts.

I rolled my eyes at the ceiling. "Guys are so clueless."

"Clueless?" He shot me a fake grimace of pain.

"Manny and Grady are getting married." I swear. I didn't know my voice was going to go up an octave, like some preteen girl at her first rock concert.

"No shit?"

"Jo-osh." I scolded. I have this thing about cussing. It hurts my ears.

"Sorry, sorry."

"Here's the best part." I poked him lightly in the shoulder. "Grady asked me to be in their wedding. I'm her bridesmaid." There went my voice again, but I couldn't help it. I'd never been in a wedding before, never even attended one. I was so stoked.

He stood and scratched his head. "Why don't they just drive up to Vegas?"

"Don't be ridiculous. Grady said they're getting married in Sedona. This June." I hugged my arms around my body. "Isn't it romantic?"

Josh tipped his head to one side, studying me.

"Grady and I went online and picked out a dress for me. And I get to have flowers and everything."

He twisted his lips together, and forced a totally weird smile. "Sure."

I shook him by the arm. "You okay?"

"Yeah, yeah."

I didn't buy it. Something was bugging him.

"No, really." He gave me a quick kiss. "I was trying to picture Manny in a tux, and I got this weird feeling." He rubbed his stomach and turned an icky shade of green.

I laughed. "It'll probably give him a weird feeling, too."

"He doesn't know yet, does he?"

"Manny proposed a couple of weeks ago, but as of yesterday he still thinks they're doing the Vegas thing."

"And you talked her out of it?"

I smiled at him proudly. "Of course I did."

CHAPTER 3

We stuck our toes in the river at Slide Rock, but the water was way too cold to go swimming. Josh stretched out on the blanket beside me, gnawing on the last piece of chicken George packed in our lunch.

With my legs crossed under me, I crunched on apple slices and stared downstream at the light reflecting on the moving water. The aspen leaves were a gorgeous bright green against the red of the canyon walls, and the creek rushed by in a soothing, Saturday-afternoon-picnic kinda way. I liked being quiet with Josh and having time to think with him close by.

He rolled over and poked me playfully in the side. "We should get our notices from the U of A this week. Think we have a chance?"

I nudged him back. "You do. I'm sure of that. You nailed your SAT's."

Josh sat up and dug through the bottom of the food bag for the last biscuit. "Grady sent your rec in?"

I nodded, but twisted my fingers together and tried to swallow the sudden nervous lump hanging out in the back of my throat. "Yeah, but the Criminal Justice degree in Tucson has such a great rep, it's full every year. I don't know. Grady says not to worry, but my mom thinks getting accepted has more to do with being lucky than anything like grades and test scores." I rolled my head back and forth, loosening my tight muscles.

Josh put his arm around my shoulder and kissed the side of my neck. "Lucky?" he whispered in my ear. Lovely little feathers of lust shivered down my spine. I closed my eyes and arched into his kisses.

He pulled me down next to him, and we cuddled on the blanket, our legs tangled together, kissing and touching. Drawing my nails in circles on his back, I snuggled closer to his heat. I closed my eyes to the speckles of sunshine glinting through the trees and felt his heart beat faster against mine. Soon we were both breathless.

His hand brushed across my face, and I gaze up at him. His eyes were dark, his face serious. "You know I love you," he said quietly, like it was a secret between us.

I kissed him softly. "I love you too."

He drew his hand along my side and pulled me closer.

Waves of heat rolled over me. I wanted him so much. My heart pounded, and I could only think about what it would feel like to be together. Really together.

"Josh," I moaned. "Please."

We froze at the sound of a car engine, and then jumped apart.

I guess it was a good thing a minivan drove up and parked just then, and those three noisy kids ran down to the water right past us.

I know my face turned so red I could have been used as a stop sign. My scalp burned. My eyes watered. I fumbled to button my shirt and busied myself with packing up the food to keep from looking at Josh or the two adults who walked by without a word.

After Josh folded the blanket, we hiked up to the

parking lot. He squeezed my hand and we laughed together, and I finally found my voice. "I can't wait until we go to college."

****

I was hanging out in Trouble's cage when Manny walked out through the back door.

"Hey, Josh." He waved and sank his hands in his pockets. Tall, muscular and confident, he had the dark eyes and straight, thick hair of his Hopi ancestry. The big, toothy grin on the cop's face had me smiling in return.

Trouble squawked from his perch near the top of his cage. He jumped down to my arm and grabbed hold with his talons. The eagle had grown steadier with his balance, and now weighed close to twenty pounds. He flapped his huge wings and watched me with his sharp, golden eyes. I handed him a piece of meat, and he gulped the food greedily.

"Congratulations," I said.

Manny rubbed his day-old beard with one hand and grinned through the chicken wire. "You heard the full story?"

"Dresses, flowers, June." I listed on the fingers of my free hand. "Forrest was floating several inches off the ground by the time she finished giving me the details."

"So I guess I should make it even," Manny said. "Wanna stand up with me?"

"Me?" I handed Trouble down to his nest and walked over to the fence. "What about the deputies you hang with? Or your buddies on the rez?"

"I've been living in Verde for so long, it makes sense to keep the important jobs in the family."

I stood there a moment and stared at the dirt floor, unsure how to react, but a warm spot glowed in the center of my chest. Family.

"C'mon, Josh. We're brothers in many ways." Manny curled his fingers through the chicken wire. "The Magician has brought us together for a reason, in this life, and in his."

I smiled and then looked up into my brother's dark eyes. I walked out the cage door and shook Manny's hand. "It'd be an honor."

With a big grin, he pounded me on the back. "I'm going to ask George to give the blessing."

"Sweet."

CHAPTER 4

I tucked the light blue cotton shirt into the waistband of my jeans and tied on my white apron. Inspecting myself in the slightly cracked mirror in the employee bathroom, I checked to make sure my hair was still neatly tied in a tight bun at the base of my neck.

With a long sigh, I fisted my hands on my hips. "So, Forrest Morgan, here you are, back scrubbing toilets at the Connor Hotel." With tourist season on the horizon, the new manager had rehired me after my summer off.

I straightened the apron bow and continued the conversation with my reflection. "Look at it this way, lucky girl." I pointed to myself. "It's only for a few more months. And if you save a little more money, you'll have enough to cover the cost of books next fall. Who knows? You might even be able to afford the occasional double latte."

I blew a long raspberry at myself. That was a mega-ton of ifs. I shifted my hips and crossed my arms. *If* I was accepted. *If* I won a scholarship. Thank goodness Mom had promised to pony up for the dorm. I smoothed the wisps of hair behind my ears. At least I wouldn't have to go into debt for a narrow bed in a tiny dorm room.

I leaned closer, shook my finger at the mirror, and

grinned. "An-n-d, if you work a couple of extra shifts, you might even earn enough for a gorgeous dress for prom night." I giggled to myself at the thought of *the* most perfect blue dress on hold in a Prescott boutique. With a happy spin, I grabbed my mop and cart. "Four rooms. I can do four rooms in no time."

Loaded to the ceiling with linens and towels and those ridiculous bottles of shampoo, I wheeled the squeaky housekeepers' cart down the hall to room six. I frowned at the old-fashioned brass number attached to the dark wooden door and blew out a quick breath. Not my fav, but I squared my shoulders and lifted my chin. If I cleaned six first, I'd get the big room out of the way. The rest of the smaller rooms would be a cinch.

The glass doorknob turned just as I put my hand up to knock. "Oh, I'm sorry." I took a step back. "The manager told me you checked out early."

Then I looked up at the guest and sucked in a holy-shit breath. A beautiful woman in an old-fashioned, full-length scarlet dress stood in the doorway. She primped the blonde curls clipped to the side of her long, graceful neck and gathered her shiny skirt in one hand. She didn't seem to notice me, so I took another step back.

My head whirled with confusion, and an army of goose bumps marched up my back. Why was this woman dressed for a Wild West show at nine o'clock on a Saturday morning? Was there another movie filming in town?

"That's a beautiful outfit." I said to be polite, but the woman didn't acknowledge my compliment, didn't even glance at me. Totally stuck-up!

Without a word, she left the room, and a wave of

knock-you-back perfume followed her down the hall. I didn't recognize the brand.

So to-tally weird. I shrugged at her rudeness. When I stepped through the door, a wall of bitter cold avalanched over me. My breath frosted, and my goose bumps grew to the size of blueberries. Frozen blueberries.

I glanced around the room, and my shoulders drooped. Oh, man, the place was a total wreck. I rushed to the old sash window, opening it to let the warm spring breeze flow into the space. Still rubbing my arms, I righted the overturned chair and bent to pick up the tangled bedclothes from the floor.

They were soaked in fresh blood.

With a shriek, I dropped the sheets, raced out of the room, and slammed the door. Breathing deeply to keep from barfing, I leaned against the wall and dug for my phone with numb fingers. Good thing Grady's number was on speed dial. Good thing she answered on the second ring.

"Captain Grady?" My voice sounded so raspy, I had to clear my throat twice. "I need to report a crime. Maybe a murder."

Deputy Stevens happened to be in Jerome at the time. Grady said she'd send him right over. By this point, I could breathe a little better, so I called down to the office, spoke to the new day manager—I think his name was Chet—and filled him in. He came up, and we waited together outside the door to the crime scene.

Manager Chet paced the hall, while I stared at the ugly pink roses woven into the carpet. In the next few minutes, he straightened his tie around his chubby neck three times. Brushing a nervous hand over his bald spot, he licked his chapped lips and muttered under his breath about wasted time.

Fiiinnnally, Deputy Stevens showed up. White male, six-one, one-ninety, blue, black, and dressed in a neatly starched Yavapai County peace officer's uniform, he tromped up the stairs and down the long, high-ceilinged hallway to room six.

"Is there a body?" He cleared his throat. He rested his hands on his jangling duty belt, probably to appear more together than I think he really was.

I shook my head. "Just lots of blood."

"See anyone leave?" When I nodded, he took out his notebook to write down my description, but a frown spread over his fleshy face while I described the lady in red.

Now I would be the first to admit the details did sound totally lame. Long, old-fashioned dress, dance hall curls, heavy perfume. Come on.

When I started describing the woman's red dress, Stevens folded his book and shook his head. "This a joke?" He glared at me, sounding super annoyed. "Captain put you up to this clever stunt?"

"No. I swear." I swallowed hard and pointed at the door with a shaky hand. "When I went in, the room felt like a freezer. I could totally see my breath. Everything was a huge mess—pictures turned sideways, furniture flipped. And blood. Lots and lots of blood all over the floor."

"Uh-huh." With one hand, he signaled for Chet and me to move a few steps back. Looking officious, he drew his weapon and opened the door.

"Aren't you going to use gloves to preserve the crime scene? This could be a big investigation." I objected. "Somebody was murdered."

Stevens grimaced at my question and marched through the door. After a long moment, he shouted, "Get in here," from the far side of the room.

I squared my shoulders, and crossed the threshold, hoping I wouldn't be sick. I glanced around quickly, and my jaw must have dropped to my belly button.

Everything was perfect. Furniture in place. Bed made. Even the fresh roll of toilet paper in the bath had its required folded point.

Stevens crossed his arms and tilted his head to the side, as if to say, what do you think you're doing, little lady, wasting my oh-so-precious time?

"I don't understand." I walked to the bed and pulled back the neatly tucked-in sheets. No body, no blood. It wasn't even cold in the room, but my goose bumps returned, big time.

Stevens punched the radio on his shoulder and reported the false alarm in a calm voice, but his body language shouted anger.

My face burned. "I-I'm sorry," I stammered. "I didn't…"

"What-ever." His eyes narrowed to slits, and he stomped toward the door. "Grady can deal with you later."

Chet whistled, long and low. "You are soooo…"

I flashed him a don't-say-it look.

"Don't know what game you're playing, Ms. Morgan, but I don't have time for this shit."

"I swear…"

He held up a pudgy hand and shook his head. "You're fired."

****

Come see me.

Captain Grady's text didn't give much away.

I leaned my head against the headrest in my jeep. Jeez. Would she be as pissed as Deputy Stevens? Or my former boss, good ol' Chet? I swallowed the cold lump lodged in the back of my throat. Would I lose my internship, too, on top of my job? Or worse, would Grady tear up my college recommendation?

I threw Tilley in gear and drove down the hill from Jerome to the police station. I didn't even race around the curves. No point in getting a ticket for speeding when I was already wading in such deep merde.

When I reached Verde thirty minutes later, I sat in Tilley and went over the weird experience in room six a dozen more times in my head. Nothing made any sense.

I rubbed my hands over my face in frustration. I saw the woman and the blood. I felt the cold. I could still smell the sickly-sweet perfume. Shivers flashed over me, and I folded my arms across my chest until the reaction passed.

I stared at the one-story station house and pounded my palms against the steering wheel. With a groan, I locked Tilley. Might as well get this over with. I entered the building, and gave a halfhearted salute to the officer at the front desk.

Without a word, he pointed toward Grady's office at the end of the hall and crossed his fingers for me.

Awesome. I shook my head in disgust. The story would be all over the station. I dragged my feet down the hall to my doom, knocked, and waited.

Grady opened the door and smiled. I shoved the corners of my mouth up…sort of. Maybe she wasn't so pissed. I crossed my fingers behind my back.

"Come in, Forrest. Sit down. I need to go find something. Be back in a minute." She patted me on the shoulder before she headed out the door and toward the file room.

I sat on the hard chair in front of her desk and stared at my hands. My heart continued to thump at double speed, no matter how many deep breaths I took in and let out slowly.

Humming a little tone-deaf tune, Grady returned in more like five minutes. I didn't complain. Might be the final five minutes I had even the micro-slimmest chance of becoming a cop someday. She hurried through the door and dumped a tattered file on her desk in front of me.

I waited silently as she pulled up a chair next to mine. "What's this?" I asked. Maybe a list of all the other interns she'd declined to recommend? I closed my eyes, unable look her in the face. Big effing list.

"Open it." She shoved the thick file closer and leaned back, looking pretty relaxed for someone who was prepping to can me.

I pushed my bangs off my damp forehead and picked up the file. Flipping through the fragile pages, I could see the earliest reports went back more than sixty years. I speed-read the cramped handwriting of reports dating from the twenties and thirties. Typed forms took over in the forties, most written in a smudged carbon-looking print. A few computer-generated pages finished the stack, but the details were similar in each report.

Here's the skinny. Beautiful woman. Red dress. Blood. Lots of blood.

Several reports mentioned the cold. A few people reported hearing a woman scream. A tourist from

Peoria named the perfume. Patchouli.

I looked at Grady, and she patted me on the shoulder. "Welcome to the crowd."

"You knew about this...phenomenon?"

"You mean Jerome's famous hotel ghost, the Woman in Red? I'm surprised you didn't. The Connor likes to publicize the fact that they're haunted."

"I don't pay much attention to tourist bunk."

"Well, tourist bunk or not, most of the deputies from the department have taken at least one report on her." Grady pointed to an interview dating back to the early eighties. "One sergeant I knew swore he heard her screams. I'm surprised the manager didn't know about the legend."

"He's new."

Grady nodded.

"Have you?" I asked. "Seen her, heard her?"

"Me? No. I don't usually handle calls in Jerome, but I sure would love to run across her sometime. Cool ghost. Your Gran never mentioned her?"

I shook my head.

"That gal does a lot to maintain Jerome's sinister ghost town rep." Her air quotes were unmistakable.

I leaned against the stiff back of the chair, and a buzzy-electricity shot of pure relief flowed through me. I wasn't crazy, or even in trouble. Best of all, I wasn't going to lose my internship, even if I had lost my job.

Grady chuckled at my obvious emotion. "You shouldn't be too surprised. You've seen other ghosts."

"I figured I saw the Magician because of Josh."

"Have you ever seen his ghost when Josh wasn't around?"

There went those goose bumps again. "Yeah,

once." I arched my shoulders forward against the chill.

"See? There you go. You're what they call a medium. Very cool."

I studied her expression closely. I'd never confessed to my little gift of reading people's thoughts, even to her. My mother knew only because she had the same gift, if you could call it that. And Josh knew, of course. I told Josh everything.

"Grady, I'm surprised you buy into this paranormal hocus-pocus."

"Didn't used to." Grady gathered the pages and reorganized the file. A reflective smile settled on her face. "Growing up in Kansas, I didn't have much experience with anything more interesting than corn. But since I've known you and Josh and Manny, well, everything's changed." She stood and tucked the file under her arm. "After all, I'm marrying a guy who works for a ghost."

CHAPTER 5

George watched from outside the pen while I feed Trouble his breakfast of two raw chickens. The bird clung to my arm and snapped up the raw flesh. He gulped down a hunk of meat and put his beak up for more.

"He's getting lazy." George said as he entered the cage. "He needs to start working for his chow."

"He's hardly ready to fly," I argued. "He can jump around on his branches, but I doubt he could get off the ground for more than a few seconds."

"He won't be able to fly for several more weeks, but he doesn't need to. Here. Give me that drumstick."

I handed the meat to George. Trouble objected, screeching the sound he always made when he was hungry.

George tied a short piece of string to the skinny end of the chicken leg and put it on the floor of the cage a few feet from Trouble. The bird watched my cousin's movements, but his talons clutched my arm through the thick leather glove I had to wear.

When George pulled the string, the chicken leg jumped a few inches. Trouble's eyes quickly focused on his prey, and he arched his wings with excitement.

George tugged the leg again. Then once more.

That was all it took. With a sharp call, Trouble jumped from my arm to the ground, his wings spread wide in an attempt to fly. He latched onto the meat with his sharp talons and began to feed.

"Call to him," George whispered beside me. "Praise him."

I screeched in the same piercing tone Trouble used. He looked up at me and beat his wings with pride. I handed him another hunk of meat as his reward.

George nodded and turned to go. "I'll talk to Homer. He can trap some rodents and rabbits for us."

"Live animals?"

"Of course. You need to train Trouble to hunt. He must be able to survive."

"But...but he won't ever..." I hesitated, trying to find the words I didn't want to think about. "Trouble will never be free to hunt," I finally managed to choke out over the lump in my throat.

"Maybe not in this world, but he will live as a free creature in the next." George closed the door behind him, leaving me and the bird to think.

Trouble thought about how he could get the last mouthful of meat off the chicken leg. I thought about how I would ever be able to... No. I didn't want to imagine... No. For now, he was my bird.

Mine to train. Mine to care for. Mine to love.

****

"I'm home, George." I dumped my backpack on the floor and dug around in the fridge for something to eat. A tough track practice had left me craving protein, so I folded half a pack of lunch meat and ate the roll in two bites. Better. A couple more packages would hold me until dinner.

I stared at the growing stack of bird books piled on the kitchen table, chose one, and flipped through the pages while I chewed. Better start thinking about my biology project if I was ever going to finish before the due date.

I headed for my room and noticed a letter on my pillow. The ham stuck in my throat, and my heart started pounding.

George must have left the envelope on my bed. I wiped my greasy fingers on the back of my jeans, picked up the large white folder, and measured its heft as I retraced my steps into the store.

At the front counter, George was finishing a credit card charge for a couple of tourists. I waited silently, shifting nervously from foot to foot while he wrapped their handcrafted basket with care and walked them to the front of the store. All I wanted to do was shove them out the door and lock it.

After he closed the door behind them, George turned with a smile on his face. "Big envelope."

I gulped for nonexistent air and nodded.

"Well, open it," he said impatiently, running a hand down one of his silver braids. "I've been waiting all afternoon for you to get home."

I rubbed my finger over the return address. University of Arizona. My heart was beating so fast I had to sit on the rocking chair by the cold potbelly stove.

My hands shook while I ripped the seal. A stack of papers and pamphlets spilled into my lap. George stood behind me and placed his hand on my shoulder.

I focused on the cover letter. "Congratulations." It began. "You have been accepted into the University of Arizona's honors medical program."

I stared at the words for a few moments, but they

didn't compute.

"Well?" George asked, "What do they say?"

"I'm in," I said quietly, and the first glimmer of excitement pierced my iced-over senses.

"Medical school? The program you wanted?"

I stood to face my cousin. "Yeah. The honors program. With a scholarship."

George threw his hands in the air and shouted with joy. He hugged me with his strong arms and yelled something like, "I knew you could do it."

I stood there in a stupor until George took me by the shoulders. "Congratulation, Dr. Kwail."

My cheeks started to heat, then my ears. "It'll be a long time before I'm even close to being a real doctor," I reminded him. Then the realization hit me, and my heart started to pound even harder. I was one step closer to my goal. My dream. And one step closer to the Magician's mandate that I become a healer.

I gave out a whoop of joy. I had to tell Forrest, but before I could, my phone beeped in my pocket, and I hurried to check the message.

"I'm in!!!"

Forrest texted. She added a happy face the size of the screen.

I grinned at George. "Forrest got her notice, too."

George usually wears this gruff-looking frown face. He's not mean or unhappy. It's just his everyday expression. But now he beamed at me, and the lines around his eyes bunched in happy creases.

The inside of my chest swirled with warmth. He was proud of me. He gave me another hug and pounded me on the back a few times. I hugged him back.

I gathered up the papers and stuffed them back in

the envelope. I would read the details later. "I need to go tell Trouble." I shouted as I ran out of the room.

****

The next morning, Forrest and I planned to meet in the parking lot before school. She drove up in Tilley and slid her ugly pink jeep into her parking spot just as I jumped off the bus. I grabbed her and swung her around in a happy circle. She was laughing and crying at the same time when I set her down again.

"I can't believe it." She caught my hands in hers. "I kept hoping and hoping, but I couldn't…"

"I know. We couldn't count on something this wonderful happening. Both of us going to the same…"

"Good news, Mr. Kwail?" Miss Abernathy walked by.

"We got in!" I was almost shouting. "I'm going to med school at the U of A."

The teacher beamed at me. She turned to Forrest. "You too?"

Forrest nodded and let out a short squeal. "U of A. Criminal Justice."

"Wonderful." The teacher grinned. "And you're accepting? Be sure to put your decision up on the senior bulletin board near the office."

****

Last night I dreamed the Magician was waiting for me in the salt mine. I had to go see him, but I waited until after George left for his Tribal Council meeting before putting my plan into action.

I circled through the numbers on the safe's combination, pushed the old brass handle, and opened the heavy door. With trembling hands, I raised the tiny seed basket from its protective wooden box and examined the finely crafted, ancient object.

I glanced at the old clock on the kitchen wall and frowned. I only had a few hours. George walked to his meeting, and fortunately, he left the keys to his truck on the kitchen counter. I chewed on my lip for a moment and then grabbed the keys, hoping he'd understand this was an emergency.

I drove as fast as I could, heading to the lonely patch of desert near the salt mines.

Down the deserted interstate.

Past the empty gas station where no one was pumping gas.

Up the narrow, bumpy road leading to the mine.

I parked near the seven-armed saguaro and hiked in the last mile. The sun set late enough now to give me light, but I had my flashlight if I needed it after dark.

I crossed the arroyo and climbed to the crest of the hill. As always, the mines were deserted, and I slid down the last hundred feet of salt-encrusted gravel to the boarded-over opening of the ancient diggings.

My markers, still in place, told me no one had disturbed my sacred site, and I quickly flicked on the flashlight and crawled through the narrow tunnel to the crystal room. I had to smile. Even Forrest, who hated dark places, liked this beautiful gift from nature.

I lit an extra lantern and sat back to enjoy the peaceful cavern. I didn't hear the Magician approach, but suddenly he was sitting across from me. Now, I know he's a ghost, but up this close, he seemed so real, so solid, I could even hear his breath.

I've spent so much time with the old spook, he doesn't scare me anymore. He's saved my life and Forrest's several times, so I count him as a friend. A friend from the Fifth world.

For some reason only he knows, he can cross over the divide between the Fourth and Fifth Worlds. He has taught me many skills, shown me many visions. They're sometimes frightening, like the water bowl filled with the beating heart of an ancient child, but he means me no harm.

The Magician held out his cupped hands, and I placed the seed basket in them. I'd already disarmed my shields, so when he closed his amber eyes, he transported me quickly to the vision place.

I stood on a high cliff and looked down at the place I call the Ruined City. I knew the time was long ago. There were no power poles in the distance, no cars driving on the highway. This was closer to the Magician's time—about eight hundred years ago.

A few people worked in the fields next to the river, but the crops were brown and lifeless. The river flowed at a trickle, like the valley had suffered from years of ferocious drought. A child played listlessly by a small fire, but most of the city seemed to be abandoned. Several walls at the top of the cliff dwelling had fallen in.

"This is after your death?"

The Magician nodded.

"Is this what happened to the people? A drought? Did they all die off? Or leave?"

I studied the tiny seed basket still resting in his hands. "Why couldn't you help them?"

The Magician pointed to an old man standing by the river's edge, his head bowed, his shoulders stooped.

"I don't understand. That's not you. I can tell by the clothes you wear now, and the eagle feather in your

hair."

I looked up, but the Magician had disappeared. He'd returned me to our cave, and the tiny seed basket sat on a rock nearby.

****

The next afternoon I told Forrest about my latest vision. We sat outside Trouble's cage and went over every detail of the mystery. I still had no clue what message the Magician wanted to convey to me. I knew the sad history of his people. Drought and war killed many of them, and forced the rest of the tribe to move farther north. Their culture was left behind, reduced to ancient ruins and broken pottery.

"Describe the man by the river again," Forrest said. "More than just his clothes. Did you see his face?"

"Only for a moment. He'd been a handsome man. Tall for his time. A strong face with deep-set eyes. But in the vision, he looked very old. No, more than that. George is old, but this man looked beaten. I think it was the set of his shoulders more than anything."

She crossed her legs under her and leaned back against the wall. "Can you imitate his posture?"

I stood and pictured the man in my memory. I copied how he stood and what he looked like. Of course, I couldn't change my face, but I imitated his expression.

Forrest had a really weird look on her face, and the skin around her mouth paled to almost blue.

"You okay?" I asked, reaching down to pull her to her feet.

"Wait. Josh. Do that again," she demanded. The tone of her voice made me even more nervous.

"What?"

"You know. His body language. His expression."

I posed again and heard her whisper "Shit," under her breath.

"Forrest. What is it?" She never curses, so this must be really bad.

She was shaking her hands like they were wet and jumping up and down in place, but she wasn't happy. She was scared. I could tell by her eyes—wide open and green, like the river on a summer day.

Her hands felt icy when I grabbed them, and she was breathing like she'd done three miles at a full sprint.

"It's him, Josh. The man by the river is Patterson, or whatever he was called back then. Don't you see? The Magician wants you to know Patterson was alive all the way back then."

I let out a long, low whistle and rubbed my chin. "That's what Zalo thought, too. That Patterson and the Magician both lived in the same time period."

I paced back and forth for a moment outside Trouble's cage. "But Patterson's not a ghost," I pointed out. "I've touched him, shaken his hand. He's solid and alive. Or at least he was last winter when he ran me off the road."

Trouble flapped his wings and screeched at me. He rose up on his wings and bumped against the top of his cage. Then he hopped over to the door, pecking at the lock like he wanted to escape.

I turned to him and spoke in a calmer voice. "It's okay, Trouble."

"He senses your emotions."

"Yeah. He doesn't like it when I raise my voice…except, of course, when I call to him for

43

dinner."

"Like boy, like bird." Forrest watched my eagle through the chicken wire and then turned to me, very serious. "You need to be careful, Josh. I think the Magician is warning you."

I gulped back the sudden rise of bile in my throat and tucked her under my arm. "Then you need to be careful, too. All of us do."

We held on to each other while she shivered. I snuggled my nose against her cheek in search of warmth.

I needed to meet with the Magician again, now. We'd figured out Patterson was the old man by the river. I needed to ask my ghost a shitload of questions. No more guessing games. Patterson tried to kill me. I needed to protect my friends and my family from this mega-creep, and I needed to know how.

I guess the Magician agreed with me, because he showed up the following night. The last time he appeared in my room, more than a year ago, he left me the courting flute.

It had to be two in the morning, although I didn't check my clock. The night was dark. With no moon, and the sky shrouded in thick clouds hiding the stars, I couldn't see across my room.

I felt his presence first, and then saw his shadow move He signaled me to follow him, and I remember walking out my bedroom door.

Then I stood on a hill overlooking Verde. I don't know how he does that, I don't even ask anymore.

Below us, the bright, colorful lights of the casino blinked into the foggy night. A few cars were scattered like dice over the large parking lot. On the weekends, the lot would be full of cars, travelers from Phoenix, and people from the Valley, all hoping to win big, but mostly going home with nothing in their pockets but despair.

The Magician held out his hand. A single red chip covered his palm. He picked it up with his other hand and broke the chip in two, handing me the pieces. He turned and walked away.

I followed him down the hill. "What do you want? I don't understand."

I stared at the broken chip. So the Magician had no use for gambling. Big deal. I pushed my hair back from my face in frustration. "Why bring me here and show me this? It makes no sense."

I woke up, shaking with cold. My blanket lay in a heap next to my bed. When I grabbed it, a broken casino chip clattered to the floor.

"But what does it mean?" I asked George for the third time the next morning.

He shook his head and slurped another sip of black coffee. "Beats me."

His answer frustrated me, but his nonchalance totally pissed me off. I slammed the chip on the table and crossed my arms.

"Look," George said after I finished growling. "You know the Magician has his own timeline. When he's ready to tell you, he'll tell you. Until then…" George put his palms up and shrugged.

I stood and paced our kitchen for a moment, then stared out the window. The symbolism of the broken chip was pretty obvious, but what did the casino have to do with the Magician and his power? Trouble squawked in his pen.

"Feed your bird." George lumbered out of the room.

CHAPTER 6

After driving home from school, I parked Tilley and trotted up the back steps to our apartment. We had a break from track practice today, and I was looking forward to a little R&R before I plowed through my stack of homework. With only four weeks until finals, I still had a major paper in Brit lit to finish.

I froze when I walked through the door and stared around the living room, slack-mouthed. The place looked like a sirocco had blown through. Piles of clothes were scattered across the couch and half-filled suitcases were strewn across the floor. The radio blared in kitchen, and the TV was turned up to full volume in the living room.

Weird. Mom hated noise.

I turned when I saw her coming from her bedroom. The worry in her expression left me feeling shaken. "What's going on?" I asked. Catching her nervousness from across the room, my heart beat a little faster.

"I'm so glad you're back," she said softly, but her voice was tight and edgy, on the verge of panic. "I was trying to pack for you, but didn't know what you'd want. We can only take one suitcase each. It's all that will fit in the car."

"Where are we going? I have school this week."

Mom glanced around the room, still distracted and frantic. Her hands kept clutching at her sides. She'd

47

pick up one shirt out of the pile on the couch and started to fold it, but then put it down and pick up another. I didn't think she heard my questions, so I grabbed her by the arms and made her look at me. "Mom, stop. Tell me what's going on."

"Shhh, he'll hear you." She stepped up closer. "I saw him. He's back." She closed her eyes and swallowed hard enough for me to see her throat work.

"Who?"

She glanced around furtively, and whispered next to my ear. "Patterson."

I moved back and eyed her with suspicion, then fisted my hands on my hips. "No way." I matched her volume, only because she was so panicked. "If Patterson was around, the media would be all over it. And besides, he's on the FBI most wanted list. The cops would have arrested him."

"He's not Patterson anymore, but it's him. I know it." She grasped my hands so hard, she hurt me. "I felt him…felt his blackness clear across the street."

"But people would recognize him."

She shook her head. "He looks completely different. Different weight, different hair color. He even appears younger, but I know it's him." Her voice had dropped to a whisper. "Forrest, we need to leave."

"Okay, okay. Here, sit down Mom. Try to calm down."

She ignored me and continued to pace, her hands in constant movement. Finally she stuffed more clothes in her suitcase, and zipped the sides closed.

"Mom," I repeated, but she didn't react.

"Mom, please," I shouted over the game show and thumping rock and roll. When she looked at me, her expression of terror doused me with cold. I sucked in a breath. "Let's call Grady. Patterson can't change his fingerprints. Or his DNA. Even if he did return, we can still prove it's him."

She stopped for an instant, rubbing her temples with her fingertips, like she was in terrible pain.

I put my hand on her shoulder, but instead of staying still, she leaped for the phone I'd just dug out of my back pocket.

"No," she shouted, even more frantic than before. Then she glanced around the room and dropped her voice back to a hiss. "You know he listens. We probably shouldn't even talk about him in here."

Remembering the cameras Patterson had secreted in our home sent more icy shivers up my back. "Let's go for a walk."

Mom nodded and grabbed her sweater from the arm of the chair. We went out the back door and down the alley. Not far from our shop, Angel's Cloud, is the tourist lookout where visitors could park to view the valley below. To the north, the red rocks of Sedona glowed in the late afternoon light. We sat on the rustic wall and watched little white clouds cast shadows across the desert floor a thousand feel below.

I pushed back a strand of my hair which was tickling my face in the light breeze. Mom was breathing more easily now. I took her hand and said in my calmest voice, "Okay. Let's think this problem through."

She took a couple more deep breaths and nodded. "Sorry. It freaked me out when I saw him."

"I totally get it. Believe me. If the guy you saw was Patterson, we need to be extremely careful."

"No phone calls," she repeated.

"What if I drive down to Verde now and talked to Grady and Manny in person?"

"He's probably bugged their office."

"Okay, we'll talk someplace safe. If Patterson has returned to the Valley, they'll find him."

Mom stared at the view, her face strained. The lines around her mouth deepened. "We should just leave Jerome. Leave the valley. No." She swallowed hard. "We should leave the state."

"Mom. I can't go now. I have important stuff at school. Track regionals are next week, and I have finals to take in order to graduate."

She pursed her lips stubbornly.

"I'm not ducking out because of that creep. He took my dad. He took you for too long." I crossed my arms and glared into the distance with her. "He's not going to take my future."

Mom stared up at the deeply blue sky. "He almost killed Josh."

"But we have the Magician watching over us. He's on our team."

She blew out a long sigh and shook her head again, listening, but hardly resigned to my argument. "I'll give Grady a couple of days to find Patterson, but we leave by the weekend if she can't. No matter what, I can't risk losing you."

I jumped off the wall and brushed the dust from the backside of my jeans. "Want to come with me to Verde? You can give Grady a first-hand description of the new and improved Patterson."

Mom smiled for the first time at my smarty-pants remark, and straightened her shoulders with more confidence. "Sure. Let's go now. But let's trade cars with Rocky so we're not quite so…"

"Obvious?" I shrugged. "I guess Tilley's pink polka dot paint job does make me stand out just a little around town."

"Just a little."

We walked back arm in arm and met Gran at the top of the stairs. "Are we going somewhere?" Gran asked, inspecting the disaster.

"Not right now," Mom said.

"Oh, that's good. I have another Tarot card reading tonight." Gran adjusted the bright pink scarf wound around her head. "I'm getting quite the reputation in town, you know. I think I might have a knack for this."

CHAPTER 7

Mom insisted Manny double-check for bugs in Grady's office. Then while she worked with the sketch artist to render a picture of the new Patterson, Manny paced the room, smacking his tight fist into his other hand. His expression grew darker and darker, the smacking louder and louder.

I sat with Grady on the far side of the room. "Your mother's right, Forrest. It would be better—safer—for all of you to leave town and hide."

I crossed my arms and scowled at her.

She put up her palms. "Just until we pick up Patterson, or whatever he's calling himself now."

"Josh needs protective custody more than anyone," I argued.

"You both do," Manny growled.

I stood, pushing back the chair with my legs. "We can't hide forever," I shouted in frustration.

Mom glanced over at me. "Forrest. They're trying to help."

I sank back on the chair. "I know."

Manny stopped pacing and stood behind Grady. He placed his hands on her shoulders, and she gazed up with him with an ooey-gooey look that made me feel just a little jealous. "Got any ideas, big guy?"

Manny nodded. "A few."

He came around and knelt down in front of me.

"Forrest, listen. You and Josh have been a huge help in solving this case."

I could hear the "but" coming. I narrowed my eyes to slits and glared at him.

"But..."

Told ya.

"...if Patterson is back, he's probably after the two of you. For some reason we have yet to figure out, he needs you out of his way. We have to keep you and Josh safe."

"Listen to him, honey," my mother said. "It's not just for you, but for Josh, and everyone else."

Grady patted my arm. "And it's not running away. It's giving Patterson more to do, so we can catch him off guard."

I folded my legs under me, rested my chin on my hands, and stuck out my lip. "I hate that horrible creep. Now we're going to miss prom night."

****

Josh was even more pissed about the plan than I was. Sitting at the kitchen table in the Trading Post, his expression turned grim while Grady filled him in.

We were to pack up tonight, and Manny would drive us to the Hopi reservation before morning. He had family there we could stay with, and rez police he trusted.

"What about my bird?" Josh threw up his arms in frustration. "I can't leave now, he's in training. And what about school?"

"We'll take care of everything." George offered. "I can watch Trouble for a few days. And we can get you excused from school."

"Finals are in *less than a month*."

"You'll be home by then," Manny assured us.

I wasn't so sure. "Listen," I pointed out. "Josh and I are the ones who've figured the clues out before. Josh is the one with the strongest link to the Magician. We all agree the spook has something to do with this whole situation, right?"

Grady nodded, and Manny eventually shrugged, but reluctantly.

"So don't bury us up on the rez. What if we go stay with Manny, out at his place, but we let it be known around town that we've booked it?"

Josh saw where I was headed and chimed in. "Then we can still help if needed, but you don't have to worry about us. We promise to stay out of sight."

I drew an X across my chest. "Promise."

****

For days later, we were still stuck at Manny's dinky ranch, and there'd still been no sightings of the morphed Patterson. Mom wrote me notes—our phones were banned. Everyone in town and at school had been told we were out in the wilds of New Mexico.

I guess it really wasn't so bad. Josh and I had lots of time together, even when we weren't studying. We took long runs up into the hills with Manny to keep in shape for track, and helped him cross-fence the upper two acres of his place over the weekend.

During the second week of our incarceration, George moved Trouble up to Manny's in the dark of night, and we installed the growing eagle in the empty barn located up the hill from the farmhouse.

Josh and I spent hours every day training the bird. Josh had decided to do his final AP research paper on Training and Care of Golden Eagles. A no-brainer in

54

my book.

Spread out in the hammock hung between two cottonwoods, I was reading my English assignment the following afternoon. The new green leaves trembled in the warm breeze. I put aside my so-totally-boring book and closed my heavy eyelids for a moment.

Josh sat by the foot of the tree, working on the leather straps he'd been crafting for days. He'd already finished the harness Trouble would wear on his legs and was now sewing a small leather hood to cover the bird's eyes.

"Forrest?" he said softly. "You asleep?"

"No," I sighed. "This book is just so boring. Jane Austen." I made a yuck-sound in the back of my throat.

Josh laughed. "I thought you liked fiction. That's why you signed up to take British lit this semester."

I gave a soft grunt.

"And you're challenging millions of Austen fans, including your teacher, Ms. Freewoman.

I opened my eyes and propped myself up on my elbows. The hammock swung beneath me. "I love challenging the status quo. And even though Austen is better than most, I like when the heroine can take care of herself, and she doesn't have to wait for some dashing hero to save her."\"No one needs to save you," he said with a straight face.

"Got that right, Kwail."

He clipped the leather thong with a knife and tied a knot at the bottom of the hood. "Finished," he declared, holding up his masterpiece for me to see. "Wanna come with me to try the hood out on Trouble?"

"Sure." I flipped out of the hammock and landed on my hands and knees in the soft green grass. We walked up to the barn, and Josh carefully opened the small side door. Trouble was now so big he needed the whole barn to move around in. After we closed the door, Josh made a chirping noise in his throat, and the bird answered from the loft. We searched the dark corners of the upper level, until Josh spotted the bird in the rafters.

"How'd he get up there?"

"Flew." Josh pulled on the heavy glove he used to hold the bird and called again. Trouble flapped his wings, but remained in the loft.

"Might have to bribe him," I whispered.

Josh shook his head. "No. He gets rewarded when he listens to me. Come on."

We left the barn and waited for a moment outside in the intense sunlight. Trouble screeched his disappointment a few times. Then we returned, and Josh held up his gloved arm. He gave his call, and the bird responded. With huge wings flapping awkwardly, the eagle dove toward the floor, landed on the horse stall nearby, and hopped onto Josh's arm with an expectant look in his big round eyes.

"Good boy." Josh rewarded the bird with a chunk of jerky and scratched his thickly plumed chest.

"He's getting huge." I moved a step closer.

"I'm guessing forty pounds," Josh said, sounding like a proud papa.

The bird eyed me carefully, but remained calm. I handed him a chunk of dried meat, and I swear the eagle smiled at me. I laughed.

"What?" Josh asked.

"He knows he's getting his lesson now."

"Sure. He's no dummy."

I studied the caged mice, lined up cafeteria style on the bench nearby and grimaced. "Do we have to use the critters again?"

Josh's turn to chuckle. "Nah. We can work on his commands with the fresh chicken legs George brought last night."

"Good," I sighed. I always feel kinda sick when a critter squeaks his last under Trouble's talons.

Josh took the eagle over to an oversized web of branches he built for Trouble to roost on. Then he dug the hood out of his pocket. Murmuring softly with words I didn't understand, he placed the hood on the bird's head.

Trouble didn't object, just stood waiting. Josh bumped his gloved arm against the bird's legs. Trouble hoped aboard, his talons tightly gripping Josh's arm.

Josh walked to the far end of the barn.

I dug a raw chicken leg out of the ice chest, tied it to the training string and placed it midway between us. Holding the opposite end of the string, I stood behind the tack room wall and peeked out between the weathered boards. The idea was for Trouble not to understand I moved the food. He was supposed to hunt, not be fed.

Josh removed the leather hood. Trouble gave a piercing screech and flapped his big wings against the quiet air. I jerked the string, and Josh gave the command in Yavapai.

Trouble studied the situation for a moment. I jerked the string again, a tiny movement this time, like a small mouse looking for a place to hide.

Eyes focused on his target, the bird left Josh's arm and buzzed the length of the barn a few feet above the ground.

One more jerk did it. With a sharp cry, Trouble dove for the prey, landing with wings spread on top of the food. Josh ran forward, removed the food from Trouble's sharp talons and handed him his reward.

I showed myself and walked across the dirt floor to meet them. "He's totally getting the idea."

"Yeah. Manny says we need to start training him outdoors. Maybe this weekend."

"Won't he just fly away?"

Josh shook his head and pulled the leather tethers from his back pocket. "Next step."

CHAPTER 8

I stared out my bedroom window at the setting sun and gave a long, deep, feeling-totally-sorry-for-myself sigh. It was prom night, and all our friends were probably getting dressed for the dance. The girls would be having their hair done at the salon in town, and all the guys were figuring out how to button their tuxes and tie their bow ties.

I leaned my head against the dusty window frame, stared at the lonely desert outside, and sniffled. The school gym would be decorated by now.

New York Night was the theme my committee had decided on, with black and gold streamers and balloons, and posters of the Big Apple for decorations. Not that anyone at our school had ever been to New York. Most of us had never been outside Arizona. The band would be setting up, doing their sound check. Parents would be bringing food.

I turned away from the window and flopped down on my single bed. Tears welled in my eyes. My pretty blue dress—the one I earned all the money for myself, after Grady got me un-fired at the Connor Hotel—hung in my closet at home. Josh would never see how awesome I look in it.

I sucked in a shaky breath. He wouldn't bring me my wrist band of flowers, or dance with me while the band played a slow song.

I flipped over onto my stomach, gritted my teeth, and pounded my fists into my pillow. I hated Patterson. If I saw him right now, I'd kick him in the-you-know-whats, and arrest him myself. I smiled at the thought of putting handcuffs on the super-creep and dragging him off to jail.

Out on the front porch, Josh and Manny laugh out loud. I growled. Probably had their boots kicked up on the railing, telling each other stupid jokes.

A truck rumbled on the gravel drive and the guys shouted hello. Grady. She hung out here a lot.

A quiet knock at my door had me sitting up, but I *did not* want to see anybody right now. I wiped the tears from my cheeks, and mumbled "Go-way."

"Forrest?" My mother's voice called softly.

I let out a long sigh. "Coming." I pushed back my messy, tear-soaked hair and answered the door.

Mom stood smiling, with Gran just behind her. Mom held my blue dress up over her head. It was so long it would drag on the floor otherwise. "Hi, sweetie. Time to get ready for prom night."

"If this is a joke, it's not funny." I crossed my arms in disgust and shot them my best eye roll. They deserved it for teasing me.

Ignoring my laser glare, Mom chuckled and pushed her way into the room. She hung the dress on the closet door and examined me from head to toe. "You better hop in the shower. Wash your hair. Gran brought her crystal clips so we can do your hair up."

"What for? We're stuck here." I threw my arms out in disgust.

"Yes, we know, dear. Just get dressed, and then we'll show you."

60

Josh poked his head through the door. "Hey, look, Forrest. Grady rented me a tux."

Still wiping the last of my tears from my face, I walked over to him and examined the zippered bag from the pricey men's store in Prescott.

"I have flowers, too." He grinned and opened the clear lid on a small, plastic box with something sweet-smelling inside.

"But…"

"We couldn't go to prom night at school," Josh explained, "so our family brought the party to us."

I glanced around at everyone's excited face. "Really?"

"Really." Gran chimed in, actually wiggling, she was so excited.

I danced around my room with happiness, but then stopped. "Oh-h-h." I groaned, covering my mouth with my hands. "I never had to time to buy shoes."

Gran held up a pink and black striped shoe box. "Found these at the church tag sale last winter. I was saving them to surprise you." She offered up the present. I noticed the Jimmy Choo name on the side. I opened the lid and my breath stopped. Literally. Under the lid sat the most totally amazing silver and crystal heels.

Gorgeous. Stunning. Incredibly, totally awesome.

I hugged Gran so tight she squeaked.

Mom shoved Josh out of the room. "Come back at seven. Not a minute before."

****

Manny struggled with my bow tie until Grady elbowed him out of the way and did it herself.

"There." She grinned up at me and patted my chest.

"You look so fabulous."

I pulled on the sleeves of the black tux a few more times and tugged at the wide, fancy belt at my waist.

"Don't mess up your cummerbund," Grady scolded. "It needs to have the wide part in the front."

I shrugged. The cucumber-thing was light blue and made of shiny material, different from the rest of the black and white tux. Something about matching Forrest.

I checked myself in the mirror one more time, and noticed my two friends staring at me with weird expressions on their faces. "What?" I asked, suddenly in a panic. "Do I have a zit?" I checked the mirror again, but my face looked okay. I let out a relieved sigh.

Manny started to chuckle and turned to Grady. "Sorta feels like our own kid, doesn't he?"

Grady's eyes turn mushy, and she hugged him.

He gave her a quick kiss and opened the door to the hallway. Grady led the way, but Manny caught my arm and pulled me back into the room. He tucked a couple of plastic squares in the pocket of my jacket. "Just in case," he said. "A man takes his responsibilities seriously."

I opened my mouth to object, but Grady called from the front room. "Come on, Josh. You've got a hot date tonight."

Manny smiled, handed me the little corsage box, and then led me through the living room.

I heard giggles and whispers from Forrest's room, but Grady marched me out the door onto the front porch and closed it behind her.

"Go on," she said, after brushing me down like a mother hen. "Knock. Like it's a real date and you're picking her up."

I rolled my eyes, but did as I was told. I was surprised to see my hand shake as I raised it and knocked twice.

Forrest's Grandmother answered the door and waved me inside. "Ohhh, nice," she said, giving me a careful inspection.

"Thanks."

"Forrest. Your young man is here," she warbled over her shoulder.

The door opened, Forrest stepped into the room, and my mouth went dry. I couldn't say anything. I just stood there like a zombie, staring at her.

Her hair was softly curled, done up in some kind of shiny clips. Her dress—oh, okay, I got it. It was the same light blue as my belt.

The soft waterfall-blue material fit her in all the right places, and gently cupped her breasts and waist. It flowed out at her feet in soft layers, and when she moved, I could see silver sparkles on her shoes. She looked up at me and smiled shyly, a light blush on her cheeks.

She was....

I gulped and attempted to swallow the cotton filling my throat.

She was beautiful. Beyond beautiful. Beyond anything or anyone I'd ever seen. My heart thumped in my chest, but it felt so good. So good to look at her and know she loved me.

"I think he's flummoxed," Gran whispered to Angela.

"Don't blame him," Manny said and gave a low whistle.

Forrest giggled and her cheeks turned a darker

shade of pink. She gave a little whirl. The dress flowed around her like a soft wind across new grass. "Do you like it?"

I nodded and managed to hand over the flowers without dropping the box.

"Thanks." she held out her hand. "Will you slip it on?"

Up close she smelled amazing. I drew in a deep breath and closed my eyes while Forrest pinned the matching flower to the lapel of my suit.

"Definitely flummoxed," Gran repeated.

I had to agree.

When all the women had oohed and ahhed over Forrest's dress and hair and flowers and even given me a compliment or two, the group led us outside. Manny pulled out a camera and snapped a few shots. The way everyone was giggling, I prepared myself for a really terrible practical joke.

Then George drove up to the porch in a sleek, old-fashioned carriage hitched with two white horses. "Where'd you get this?" I asked.

He tipped his hat up so I could see the grin on his face. "Knew somebody who knew somebody."

Forrest kept making little happy noises in the back of her throat.

I handed her into the seat of the carriage, and George clicked his tongue against his teeth to set the team in motion. Gran and Angela waved good-bye. "See you tomorrow." Angela called.

We were off.

Where? I didn't have a clue. But it had to be better than sitting on the porch telling stupid jokes while Forrest cried in her bedroom.

I smiled over at her, and she beamed up at me. She held my hand tightly and bounced with excitement on the seat. "Did you know about this?"

"Nope. Pretty awesome, though."

"Where…" She didn't get to finish her question. We had pulled around the back side of the barn and under the cottonwood trees was…

****

"…the most beautiful, most romantic setting I've ever seen." I let out a happy sigh and gazed up at Josh. Someone had hung sparkle lights in the trees, and set up a table for two in the middle of the grassy lawn, complete with a long white table cloth, and candles and everything. A painted wooden platform was dressed up to look like a dance floor, and a boom box stood nearby on a small table.

Real wine glasses of something bubbly sat on the table, and china and silverware gleamed in the last of the evening light. There were even flowers. Just like mine. Little white roses and silver ribbons. I thought my heart would break, it was so pretty. Like a dream.

"I guess we're going to Prom." Josh grabbed me by the waist and lifted me out of the carriage.

"Better than prom." I whirled in a circle, arms out, giddy with the awesomeness of what our families had done for us. "Who needs a gym filled with balloons?"

With a quick salute, George snapped the reins and drove off with the horses and carriage. We had the place to ourselves. Quiet music played now, but I bet there were some hot tunes to dance to on the play list.

Josh offered me his arm, and we walked across the cool grass to the table. He even pulled out my chair when we sat down. He sniffed the golden liquid in his glass.

"Champagne?"

"Cider."

I didn't care. I just wanted to sit here and look at everything. I wanted to remember this moment for the rest of my life. I guess my eyes started leaking, because Josh got a worried look on his face and took my hand.

"No, really. I'm okay." I assured him with an enormous smile. "Happy tears, you know?"

He glanced around. "Do you think they'll bring us some food?"

I heard footsteps in the grass and turned to see Grady and Manny carrying silver-covered trays. They were dressed in dark clothes covered with fresh white aprons. I clapped my hands happily, like a little kid, when they put a scrumptious-looking meal in front of us. It smelled totally amazing.

"Mademoiselle," Manny said, in a pretend-snooty voice. He centered my dish in front of me, lifted the silvery lid to release heavenly smells, and placed a linen napkin in my lap.

"How?" I started to ask.

Manny shrugged and shot me a crooked grin. "We asked someone who knew someone." Then his expression went serious. "Your mom and grandmother left already. George is taking the rig back to his friend's place, but Grady and I will be in the house if you need anything. No one knows you're here, but here's a phone in case of an emergency."

"We'll be fine," Josh assured him, and Manny nodded.

Grady placed our desserts to the side, but then bent to whisper in my ear. "If you need protection, it's under your plate."

My cheeks burned, and I opened my mouth to object, but Grady put up her hand. "A young woman always takes care of herself."

I glanced over at Josh, but he hadn't seemed to notice the conversation, and I let out a relieved breath.

I was too excited to eat much, but Josh finished every bite, of course. There was even chocolate cheesecake. I knew where that came from. The Haunted Hamburger.

In the west, the sunset turned from yellows to oranges to deep reds and glorious purple. The stars came out. The music played. I was in heaven. We danced so much, I had to take my shoes off.

Josh hung his coat on his chair, and I helped him out of his cummerbund. I smiled at him shyly while I undid his bow tie. I couldn't stop thinking how handsome he was, how wonderful. When he kissed me, my breath caught, and my heart raced in glorious circles.

The night was warm, almost sultry, and off in the distance thunder rumbled over the Verde River. Josh grabbed his coat, laid it out on the soft grass, and we sat together, relaxed and happy, and watched the lightening glow in the distant clouds. The breeze blew the sweet, rainy smell of the desert toward us.

I sighed, a really deep, long sigh of perfect contentment, and Josh put his arm around me. When he nibbled on my neck, my pulse raced faster. I arched toward him, closed my eyes and waited for him to kiss me on the lips.

Oh, his kisses were so sweet, but they heated quickly. I opened my mouth. We played touch with our tongues, until I was having trouble finding air. His hand tightened around my waist.

I moved back just a breath. "Josh?"

"Humm?" he said between the kisses he trailed down the side of my face and over my ear.

"Is this the right time?"

He pulled back and looked into my eyes.

God, I wanted him. It was tough to breathe.

He touched my face with his palm, and I cuddled my cheek into it.

"I love you, Forrest. I want you more than anything, but are you sure?"

My heart was beating so hard, I could hardly think straight. With a smile, I cuddled up next to him, and held open my arms. He didn't hesitate, but covered me with his body and deepened the kisses. I could feel the tension rippling through him, feel the heat of him. I combed my fingers through his hair, and he moaned into my mouth.

CHAPTER 9

The light of dawn woke me, and I stirred carefully, hoping not to wake Forrest. She curled onto her side, and I covered her with my jacket.

I wanted to stroke her hair, feel her warm skin under my hands, but I resisted. Instead, I stood and walked the short distance to the dance floor to shut off the music still cycling through on the CD. I straightened my shoulders, smiled to myself, and let out a long sigh. There would never be another night like last night.

"Josh?" Forrest whispered behind me, and I turned. She clutched my jacket around her shoulders.

"You okay?" I held out my arms, and she walked into my embrace. We held each other in silence for a long moment. I stroked her soft hair.

Then she grinned at me. "I'm so happy."

I must have looked relieved, because she laughed softly.

"I was…"

"…worried?"

My ears heated. "Well, yeah. I was worried about you. About how you would feel, now …"

She moved her arms up around my neck and smiled at me in a seductive way. "Now that we're lovers?"

I combed my fingers through her tangled hair and gazed into her deep blue-green eyes. Not a trace of regret showed on her beautiful face.

"I love you, Josh. It was the right time. The right place."

"I love you too." I hugged her closer and blinked away a nervous tear I never want her to see.

"Come on," I said after I could speak. "I'm starved. Let's go see if anyone is up."

I could smell of bacon and toast from the front porch, and my stomach started to growl. When we walked into the cabin, Grady gave us a quick wave. Forrest headed for her room, but I gave Grady an everything's-cool smile and sat at the small kitchen table.

Grady popped in two more slices of sourdough in the toaster and turned to study me seriously. She crossed her arms and leaned against the counter. "Did you use it?"

I dodged her look and ignored the question by fiddling with the napkins and silverware on the table.

"Josh, were you careful?"

I cleared my throat. Of course I knew what she was talking about, but having a conversation with the police chief about safe sex had me squirming in my seat.

****

"Of course we were careful," I said from my doorway. "Thank you, Grady. Manny gave Josh some condoms, too."

"Good. Manny's idea, but I agreed. So did your mother. We asked her permission."

I walked across the room and kissed Grady on the cheek. "Thank you for watching out for us."

Grady put her hands on my shoulders and tucked her chin. "Everything okay?" she asked in a super-serious tone.

My cheeks heated, but I looked straight at her. "Glorious," I said firmly, glancing at Josh.

He grinned back at me.

After Josh ate an enormous breakfast, we slept, cuddled in the hammock, most of Sunday. A deeper sense of closeness surrounded us, and we caressed each other softly even while we slept. I'd never felt so content.

It was getting dark by the time we wandered back to the house arm in arm. Grady stood on the front porch, looking down the road towards the front gate.

"Manny back yet?" I called from across the driveway.

Grady yanked on her short ponytail and frowned. "Haven't heard from him." She turned and went back into the cabin, letting the screen door slam.

Josh and I gave each other worried glances and followed.

"I thought he was supposed to be back by noon," I said as we both entered the cabin. "Did he call and tell you he'd be late?"

Grady shook her head and paced the small room with her hands on her hips. "I've called his phone a dozen times. It keeps going to voice mail."

I tried to swallow the prickles in the back of my throat, but couldn't. "Weird."

I hurried across the room to Grady and put an arm around her shoulder. She wasn't trembling, but she sure was tense. "Maybe he's out of range. Maybe his battery died in his phone."

Grady stared up at the ceiling. "Yeah maybe, but I can't shake the bad feeling in the pit of my stomach."

"Have you called your office yet?" Josh asked. "Made a missing persons report?"

"Too soon for any official report." Grady shook her head and went back to pacing. "Besides, he'd be furious. But I have a few guys out combing the hills."

A car horn beeped in the distance, and we rushed out the front door with relief, but it wasn't Manny. Mom drove Gran up to the house in her old wreck of a car, leaving a dusty trail behind them.

Mom hopped out the driver's seat and helped Gran up the steps. They both looked worried, their faces taut with concern. No, worse than that. They looked totally shit-scared. My heart thump-thumped in my chest, and I couldn't dislodge the eerie feeling still clinging to the back of my throat.

We followed them through the screen door and gathered in the main room. Grady filled them in on Manny's disappearance.

"Tell everyone what you read," Mom said to Gran.

Gran looked flustered. Her short gray hair stuck out from the bright blue turban wrapped around her head. She clutched and re-clutched her hands in front of her, glancing at each of us in turn. "I brought the cards to show you."

Mom helped her to the kitchen table, and we all gathered around.

"I was working with my new deck...my Tarot cards." Gran explained with a quiver in her voice. "I was...I was practicing for a reading I'm doing tomorrow. I wanted to do the spread called the Celtic Cross, but you know, I was just playing with the deck, and remembering what each of the cards represents, and how they're related to one another."

I took the chair opposite her and could see how much her hands were shaking. Patting her arm, I smiled into her worried face. "It's okay, Gran."

Blinking rapidly, she pinched her lips together. Her eyes were wet between the soft wrinkles, but she continued to stroke the beautifully decorated cards.

I've never paid much attention when Gran does her Tarot readings, but right now I wanted to know what each of the cards meant, and why my mother was so upset.

"I wasn't thinking about anyone in particular. I wasn't worried, so I asked the deck, 'What is of the utmost importance for me to know about myself and those who matter in my life?'"

The first card quivered in her hand as she began with a pattern I'd seen her use before.

She laid it in the center of table and pointed, "This was the first card."

XII, The Hanged Man lay faceup on the table, and a chill swirled over my shoulders and into my heart. Behind me I heard Grady gasp.

This couldn't be good.

Gran continued in a somber tone. "This position in the center of the spread tells me who the reading is about. *The Hanged Man* represents one who makes a sacrifice. You can see he is turned upside down."

Josh put his hand on my arm and squeezed lightly. I took hold and squeezed back.

"He sees life from a different point of view than others involved. This person has divinatory powers, wisdom, and intuition. He usually has the gift of prophecy."

"Is this you?" I whispered.

Gran shook her head.

Josh took a deep breath and swallowed hard. "It's Manny." Gran glanced up, her face pale. "I wasn't sure before, but maybe I should have been. Yes, I believe this card represents Manny. He has this kind of power. I do not."

Slowly she drew the second card from the deck and laid it crosswise over the *Hanged Man*. "This is what crosses the subject. It brings energy to surround the situation. It could be reinforcing energy or opposing energy such as obstacles, challenges, or a warning of what could stand in one's way."

"This is *XVI, The Tower*," my mom whispered, pointing to the picture of a windowless stone structure being struck by a bolt of lightning. People were falling to the ground from the top of the tower.

Gran held up her hand. "I must do this."

Graciously, Mom conceded and sat back, but she continued to frown.

"*The Tower* means major change, adversity, and misery. It has to do with a significant restructuring of one's life, or an overthrow of an existing way of life."

"But it means life, doesn't it?" Grady asked. She moved around the small table and took a seat next to Gran. The four of us clasped hands for a moment— Gran, Mom, Grady and me.

"There is change coming," Gran whispered. "And I believe, because *The Tower* is so strong, it could mean change for all of us."

Gran broke our circle of hands and reached for the third card. She placed it beside the first two, closer to her. "This position near me is the far past. It can often be attributed to the foundation or root of the situation, but sometimes it's the hidden root or influences from the distant past."

I leaned forward. *The King of Swords*. I read the words softly.

Gran closed her eyes for a moment and resettled her body. She took a deep breath and let it out slowly. "The *King of Swords*, when it's upside-down like this, and placed in this direction, has to do with cruelty and evil intentions."

Patterson. The name echoed in everyone's mind. My heart pounded with fear for Manny and Grady. For all of us.

"Yes. This is Patterson." Her voice quivered. "He's a person in a position of authority who makes unlawful judgments and decisions."

"There are storm clouds in the background," Josh said.

When he withdrew his hand to point out the storm clouds, I immediately felt colder, and very much alone.

He paced the room for a minute, and Gran waited with the next card still hidden in the deck. "We all realize Patterson's intentions are evil."

Josh pushed his fingers through his hair and rejoined the group. "Do you believe this?" he asked me, gesturing to the cards in front of us.

I huffed impatiently and faced him. "Do you talk to ghosts? Do my mother and I hear people's thoughts? Does Manny appear out of nowhere when we need him?"

I turned back. "Gran. What comes next?"

She turned over the card and my shoulders relaxed. "That's us, isn't it?"

Gran smiled across the table at me. For once. "Yes.

And in this position, *Two of Cups* is the counterbalance to the negative influences of the recent past."

"See Josh? We're the contrast," I said with hope.

Gran nodded, her voice stronger, her face more relaxed. It was as though she—and we—had gotten through the awful part. "This lion has the wings of spirit, indicating a good balance between spiritual and earthly love. The card shows the beginning of a new romance, or a well-balanced friendship. The young lovers, a youth and a maiden, are pledging to each other."

My cheeks heated, remembering our night together.

Gran set the card above the *Hanged Man*.

"Is that the future?" Grady broke in.

"Yes, but more like a message or an invitation. This placement represents what could possibly happen." Then came the *Knight of Cups*, and Gran placed the card carefully to the right in the square she was building.

Grady leaned closer, and we all studied the young man riding over a peaceful green field. He held a cup in his hand. In the distance, a quiet river flowed through a green meadow.

"He wears a winged helmet." Gran tapped the card. "The sign of imagination. And he is graceful, not warlike."

"Is this Josh?" Grady asked.

Gran wrinkled her brow. "I don't know. That is for the future to show us. Even though the picture is of a boy, it could be anyone."

"Wait." Mom covered Gran's hand with hers before she could draw another card. Her eyes made contact with each of us. "Before you see this next card, I want you to know it doesn't always mean exactly what it says."

"No, but it usually relates back to the person the reading concerns."

"Manny?"

"This card foretells the near future." A tear trickled down Gran's face as she turned over *XIII, Death*.

Oh, God. Number thirteen. I gasped, and so did Josh.

Grady closed her eyes.

"This card indicates the destruction of the old, and transformation followed by positive change, rebirth and renewal."

Mom took hold of Grady's hand. "Wait, Grady. This card doesn't mean Manny's dead. You have to believe us. It only means bone-deep change is coming."

"But it could mean death?" Grady whispered.

Silence filled the small room. Nobody argued against the possibility.

Josh pointed to the card. "It could mean Patterson will die."

Grady pushed back from the table and stood. "I need to get to the office. We need to start a search for Manny, now."

"Hold on to hope, Grady." But could I do that myself?

CHAPTER 10

I checked the old clock on the wall for the hundredth time and tried not to let my mounting anxiety show. Forrest shot me a what-do-we-do? look. Manny was now more than eight long hours overdue.

Officer Boyd arrived and was assigned to guard Forrest and me. Angela and Gran stayed with us, too. Grady took off for her office in Verde just after dark.

Rifle resting across his shoulder, Officer Boyd paced the wooden porch outside. Inside, we waited in silence until George, who'd been at the Trading Post, returned to the ranch late that night to give us the news. Or lack of it.

The deputy tipped his hat as George mounted the wooden steps and clumped across the porch to the door. We all stood, hoping for good news, but the look on my cousin's weary face warned of heartbreak. Angela put her arms around her mother. Forrest clung to me.

He swiped his hand across his mouth. "Grady ordered a search party. When the call went out, most of the deputies on the force showed up within an hour."

I nodded. Even though Manny wasn't technically a member of the sheriff's office, he was well liked and highly respected.

"And two hours later, they found his truck." George whacked his dusty hat across the side of his leg and hung his head. He drew in a very audible breath.

"Is he okay?" Forrest asked in a whisper.

"Don't know. Lots of blood."

Forrest moaned at the word, and my stomach dropped to my knees.

George swallowed hard. "No track marks, or tire marks. No…body."

"No body? That's good, then. No body." Forrest chimed in, ever the optimist.

I squeezed her trembling shoulder. "Maybe he's hiding," I suggested. I didn't believe it, but hoped everyone else would.

"Maybe someone helped him get away. Maybe…" Forrest's voice cracked, and she moaned again softly. Turning to me, she hid her face in my shoulder.

Forrest started to cry, and her tears soaking my shirt didn't help me keep it together. I choked up and couldn't say much for minute. All I could do was hold onto her. I squeezed my eyes shut to fight back my own tears.

Gran gave a trembling moan, and Angela helped her back to the couch, where she sat holding the old woman's hand.

George walked slowly across the room and eased himself into a kitchen chair. He appeared older and more tired than I'd ever seen him.

Gran sniffled in the corner. "I'm so sorry," she said to the group. "If I hadn't…

Forrest straightened her shoulders. "This is not your fault, Gran. This is because of that creep Patterson."

Angela nodded. "We need to get out of here. Now."

Forrest shook her head and leveled her gaze. "No.

There's nowhere to run. Don't you see, Mom? What chance do we have against this guy if even Manny couldn't stop him?"

I had to agree, although the knowledge left me numb. "We have to figure out what Patterson wants, and then work together to put this guy where he belongs."

George rubbed his thumb and finger against the bridge of his nose. "No jail could hold him."

Cold fear shivered down my spine, but I felt a rush of knowing, a powerful conviction, and stood up, looking into the eyes of each person in the group. "Then we send him to the Fifth world, where he should have stayed eight hundred years ago."

****

Josh paced the living room floor for more than an hour. He finally turned to me and, with a quick nod of his head, signaled me to follow him to his bedroom. Bright moonlight glowed through the front window.

We tiptoed past Gran and my mom, both asleep on the couch. George still sat at the kitchen table, but didn't say anything when Josh quietly closed the door to his room.

He took my hands in his. "I need to go find the Magician."

"At the salt mine?"

He nodded, searching through a pile of clothes on the floor for his jacket.

"Want me to come with you?"

With a quick glance at his alarm clock, he shook his head, and then took me into his arms. "No. If I leave now, I can get there by morning. You stay here. Try to keep everyone calm."

"Yeah, right."

The sound of the deputy's heavy boots pacing the wooden porch outside reminded me of one more adult we would have to avoid if Josh was going to get away from the ranch.

Josh tipped his head toward the sound. "Can you handle him?"

I reached up and pulled Josh tight to me. Breathing in his scent. Remembering the way he felt in my arms. He held on to me like he never wanted to let me go, while his heart raced against mine. He bent to kiss, me and I clung to him.

"Be careful." My cheeks were wet when he took me by the shoulders and gently pushed me back.

"I'll be back here by noon." He moved over to the back window and quietly raised the sash.

I blew him one more kiss and closed the door behind me. My job—distract Deputy Boyd.

I poured a fresh cup of coffee and took it with me to the porch. "Heard anything yet?" I asked, holding out the mug. It steamed in the cool night air.

After putting down his rifle, Boyd accepted the coffee, blew on it, and huffed out a disgusted snort. "Nothin'. Grady won't let us use our radios or phones. We're under orders to stay put and wait until we get word directly from her."

Even though my heart was pounding in my throat, and I could hardly speak, I sat on the porch rail and pretended to be relaxed.

I drew little circles with my finger on the beam next to me. "So, how's your new little kid?"

"Sammy?" Boyd's expression relaxed just a fraction. Then his smile widened to a grin. He dug in his pocket for his phone. "Ah, he's great. Growing so fast. See?" the officer scrolled through his pictures. He held the phone out for me to see the pictures of his son. "Here he is a month ago. And here's one from last week."

"Wow." I exclaimed a little louder than I might have at the blond-haired, bright-eyed baby. "What a cutie. And how big he is already."

Boyd swelled with pride. His shoulders rose and his eyes crinkled with an even broader smile. Taking back the phone, he stared at his young son lovingly. "Already fifteen pounds."

"At three months?"

"Yep. Amy calls him our Baby Bruiser."

"Amazing." I swung down off the rail and stared across the dark desert. Josh was probably a mile from here already. The sinking feeling in my stomach made me wince, but I couldn't let on. *Stay cool, girl.* "Well, think I'll try to rest. It'll be daylight in a couple of hours. Good night."

Boyd shot me a quick salute and returned to his watch.

The screen door squeaked when I opened it, and I tiptoed to my room. Gran snuffled in her sleep, and I smiled in spite of my fear. Night air breezed in through the curtains, spiced with the minty smell of creosote. I closed my window and sank my face into my pillow and fought to hold back my tears.

****

Grady was so totally pissed the next morning. She finally showed up at the ranch around six, and when Boyd filled her in on Josh's escape, she looked ready to strangle the deputy. She turned him inside out for not doing a better job of guarding Josh.

I came out of the house to interrupt her. "It's my fault, Grady. Josh needed to leave. I helped him."

Grady looked like hell. As she grabbed me by the arms, her face reddened. "Are you two out of your minds?"

George took her by the shoulders and gently drew her away. "Josh needed to go."

Grady clamped her jaw, growled something like "idiots" and slammed out of the house. She jumped in her truck, spun the back tires in the dirt, and roared down the dusty road back toward town.

Standing behind me, my mother put her hands on my shoulders and gently kneaded her fingers down my arms. "She's scared."

I leaned into Mom's comfort and tried to take a deep breath. My eyes blurred with tears. "Me too."

CHAPTER 11

I reached the mines just after sunrise, exhausted from the run. Skidding down the last hill, I ripped the rotted boards covering the entrance aside and crawled as quickly as I could toward the crystal cave. I was so thirsty I gulped two bottles from my stash and started a third.

"Where are you?" I shouted when I had enough breath.

Damn ghost.

I sat on the floor to wait. My heart finally slowed, and I wiped the sweat off my face with the front of my T-shirt.

Fortunately, it wasn't long before the Magician showed his face. He stood calmly before me.

If I could have punched the guy, I would have. I threw the empty water bottle against the wall. "Stop this," My angry shout echoed around the chamber. "Stop playing games. Stop letting people..." I choked on the word.

I squeezed my eyes shut to hold back the stinging tears. I had to fight to contain my anger, or I wouldn't be able to communicate with this damned old spook. I sucked in a long breath of salt air and waited until my heart slowed. I clamped my hands together against my thighs to force myself back under control.

Finally, I could breathe again. Think again. I folded

my legs under me and sat in the stillness. When I closed my eyes, the Magician took me.

We stood on the hill above the casino. I could tell from the Magician's rigid stance that he was angry. He fisted his hand and raised it to the bright lights that gleamed below us, his face a mask of fury. His craggy face was grooved with deep, angry furrows.

I through my hands in the air. "What do you want? I can't do anything about the casino. The tribe owns it. It makes money for the people."

The Magician narrowed his eyes to angry slits. The scene changed. In a flash, the colored lights dimmed, and only a bonfire remained. The Magician pointed down the hill, and I moved forward alone.

In the light of the fire, I watched the man who had been the Magician. He was wearing full ceremonial regalia, a fine red cloak covering his shoulders, and a strange, rounded hat perched on his head. The cat necklace, the one he'd given me, hung from his neck.

I'd never seen the Magician dressed this way before, but the difference was in more than the clothes he wore. He saw beyond this night, beyond the bonfire, beyond me.

A half-grown native boy who couldn't have been more than ten stood next to him, holding the sacred seed basket and the Aztec water bowl. Since he was partially turned away from me, I couldn't see the boy's face, but recognized both objects as the Magician's tools. My tools.

A man lay near the fire on a pallet of deer skins. He was obviously ill, his body thin, his face gaunt. The man moaned and clutched his side.

From out of the darkness, another man emerged,

carrying a long spear horizontally in his two hands, like a sacrifice. Dressed only in a loincloth, he walked around the fire and moved slowly toward the others. He turned to face me, and the fire lit his features.

I sucked in a breath and blinked a few times. I would have known the face anywhere. "Manny," I shouted, reaching for him.

He didn't seem to hear me. Didn't acknowledge me.

Even when I called his name again, Manny didn't turn to look at me. Somehow I could see what was happening, but couldn't participate. Couldn't be seen or heard by my ancestors.

Hands clenched, I stepped back and waited. Patience. George always harps at me. Patience.

A full moon lit the scene. Manny set the lance before the Magician. Now I could see three large eagle feathers attached to the leather-bound handle.

The Magician circled the fire four times. I held my breath and stood perfectly still. I could swear I heard a low hum. I looked around and angled my head to listen more closely. The sound wasn't a voice. It wasn't made by the ancient men who stood before me.

I closed my eyes, listening more intently. The hum reverberated around me, through me, an energy I'd never felt before. I raised my palms from my sides and threw back my head to stare at the sky.

The sound came from the earth and filled me, reverberated in the depths of my body. My soul. I rubbed my chilled arms. Was this the source of the Magician's power?

The Magician took something from the seed basket and sprinkled it on the chest of the sick man. Then he knelt and dripped blood from the bowl onto his forehead. The man on the pallet relaxed, his pain eased. He closed his frightened eyes.

Manny raised the weapon, and the energy surrounding us called to the wind. A roaring, howling storm overtook us. I could no longer see.

I awoke in the crystal cave. Alone. The lance lay across my outstretched hand. I picked it up and ran all the way back to Manny's ranch. Instead of taking the roads, I cut across the desert to save time, but I was exhausted from the heat of the morning sun by the time I reached the ranch.

****

"We need to investigate the casino," I told Forrest in between gulps of my third glass of water.

"We don't have a computer," Forrest complained. "We'll need to contact Grady, get the FBI started on this."

"But how will you explain it?" Angela asked.

"Grady's going to jump on any clue at this point," I argued. "Besides, she knows we want to help. The Magician wants to help, too."

"What's with the spear?" Forrest asked, taking the finely carved wooden weapon from me. "A new gift from your ghost?"

"That and more."

She examined the pointed end closely and looked up at me. "It used to have something attached here."

"I know." I dropped my chin. "Eagle feathers."

"Now?" Her voice squeaked.

I shook my head once. "No. We don't have time."

George dug in his pocket for his keys. "You two go find Grady. Take my truck. I'll take care of things here until you get back."

Angela looked panicked. "No." She grabbed Forrest by the wrist. "The kids should stay here. They should hide. If Manny couldn't…"

"There's no point in hiding, Mom," Forrest gently pulled her arm back. "Patterson knows where we are. He's probably known all along. Whatever's going to happen, has to happen. We couldn't stop it even if we hid on the moon."

Angela glanced at George, and when he nodded, she sat back on the couch and buried her face in her hands.

Gran looked terrified and reached for me. "You will be careful, won't you?" Her voice sounded thin, and old, and helpless.

Forrest gave both women a hug and walked toward the door. George tossed me the keys, and I took Forrest's hand. His truck was hidden behind the barn, and we walked up the hill together in the morning heat. Forrest still carried the spear.

Trouble must have heard us coming, because he called to me in his high screech as we passed the barn. I hesitated, but Forrest tipped her head toward the door and smiled. "Go see him."

We entered the cool space, and the dusty smell of old hay tickled the back of my throat. I pulled the training glove on and called to my bird. After he landed on my arm, he looked expectantly at both of us for food. His large golden eyes blinked, as he turned his head to study Forrest.

She held out a chunk of jerky, and I must have looked surprised. "I always carry some in my pocket now, just in case," she explained, as she feed the bird a second hunk.

The bird took the food from her hand and swallowed, looking around immediately for more. "Greedy Gus," cooed Forrest, handing over another chunk. She stroked the bird's chest. "But you have to trade this time."

Without warning, she took hold of the bird and pulled two large feathers from his tail. The bird squawked and beat his wings against my shoulder.

"What the…" I cried out.

Forrest held up her hand. "A small sacrifice for the cause." She gave the bird a large chunk of dried meat. "Come on. We have an important meeting."

CHAPTER 12

I drove while Josh attached the eagle feathers to his new spear with a length of leftover leather thong I grabbed from the workbench. He hadn't said a word since we climbed in the truck. I know he wanted to do this work right, but there was more to it. "Josh?"

"Yeah?"

"You pissed at me?"

He shook his head, but didn't look me in the eye. I felt a little sick, and swallowed hard to keep my throat from closing up completely.

He gave a long sigh, one I could hear over the roar of the truck engine barreling down the highway. "I'm not angry with you. Confused. Yes. The Magician is being so mysterious. I still don't know what he wants."

"He's obviously not happy about the casino."

"Right. There's something about the place. Something he needs back."

"Do you think the area is a vortex? A place that has to do with his power? Maybe the source of his power?"

Josh stared out the window, his jaw tight, his eyes narrowed in concentration. I didn't have to read him to know he was remembering. Probably going through every vision he'd had with his old ghost since he was a kid. Without looking down, he drew his hand along the silky edge of the eagle feathers now attached with a leather thong to the ancient spear. "I know it's a healing place."

"Whoa." A shiver skittered up my spine. "Could be related to all the tools he's given you?"

"Could be. In the last vision, the tools were all there." He pushed back his hair. "Except for the flute."

I gulped again and clenched the steering wheel. "Am I the flute?"

We glanced at each other. Josh nodded and leaned his head back against the headrest. He licked his lips like he was thirsty, but the color on his face had changed. Kinda green.

I parked the truck in front of the sheriff's office and yanked the brake after turning off the engine. Josh sat up and stared at me for a moment.

"Forrest." His voice was rough, parched. Scared. "You should go."

I shook my head in confusion. "No way. We need to talk to Grady…"

"No, I mean you should take your Gran and your mother and leave Verde. You know what the cards said."

"Listen. I don't know whether to believe Gran's reading. She could be…"

He gave me a you've-got-to-be-kidding glance and scooted across the long seat, taking my hands in his. "You believe in my ghost. You can read the truth in other people. Your mom can, too."

"That's different."

"It's not. It's all part of the same thing. Part of something we don't fully understand, but I won't be able to do what I need to do if I have to worry about you. Patterson…"

"Wants to destroy you," I growled through

clenched teeth. "I'm not going to stand back and let him take…" I swallowed hard, "the man I love."

Josh hugged me closer. I was sure he was crying, just like I was. My heart was pounding next his, and I heard him suck in a jerky breath.

"I can't let you go," I sobbed. "Please, Josh. I'm the flute. I'm part of the whole mystery. Your ghost comes to me, too. Remember? He helped me save you."

Grady stood outside the front door of the sheriff's office. I don't know how long she'd been there. I don't know how much she'd heard, but I jumped out of the truck and ran to her. "Tell him," I shouted. I didn't care who heard my desperate pleas. "Tell him I can help. Tell him…tell him we have to do this together."

****

The Magician stood on the hill behind me. My head ached with the hum of the vortex, and my heart pounded painfully in my throat.

"I have to go." I could barely choke out the words.

Forrest put out her hand and called to me, but I couldn't hear her voice.

I didn't want to leave her like this, but I didn't have a choice. I walked away from George's truck and waved to the Magician, who still standing in the distance.

I hesitated and turned to look into her face. More than anything, I wanted to hold her once more, but if I went to her now, if I took even one step toward her, I wouldn't be able to leave her side, and I'd never fulfill my destiny.

The tears on her face burned in my heart. "I love you," I said and grabbed the spear.

****

92

The eagle feathers twisted in the breeze as Josh walked away.

My knees buckled, but Grady held me upright. Blinded by tears, I bit my lip to keep from calling out his name.

I couldn't hear what Grady was saying over my sobs, but I know she wanted to comfort me. How she had any comfort left to give with Manny lost or hurt or dead, I couldn't fathom, but we stood on the porch together and watched Josh break into a trot, climb the hill nearby and disappear over the ridge.

I could see the faint outline of the Magician in the distance. They were heading north, toward the casino.

Grady led me through the door and into the hall. The air conditioning chilled the tears on my cheeks. I washed my face in the ladies' room sink and placed cool towels over my bloodshot eyes. I choked back one last round of tears and finger-combed my hair into a knot.

Leaning my hands against the cool sink, I sucked in a breath and stared in the mirror for a long moment. I gritted my teeth and slowly sucked in air through my nose to calm myself. Okay, so maybe I couldn't follow Josh. Maybe I couldn't be a part of whatever ceremony that stupid ghost had in mind, but I could find out what all this hocus pocus had to do with the casino.

I straightened my shoulders. Purpose gave me sudden strength. I would help Josh the way I knew how. I slammed out of the bathroom and headed down the hall toward Grady's office.

I glanced in through the glass window. A meeting with two FBI guys up from the Phoenix office had just broken up. Solemn-faced, they shook hands with

Grady, hurried past me, and marched in unison out the front door of the station.

When I walked through her office door, Grady looked even more worried than before. I approached her desk. "Any luck finding Manny?" I asked, pretty much seeing the answer on her stricken face before I finished the question.

She shook her head. "Since Manny is…" she sucked in a quick breath, "…a federal officer, the FBI is taking over the search. I've had my deputies combing the desert, starting at Manny's truck and moving out from there. No luck. But still no…" she swallowed hard and clenched her fists. "No evidence."

Neither of us wanted to say the word. Or even think it.

"Josh has another clue from the Magician."

Grady looked up, hope sparking in her eyes. "Did it have something to do with the spear he took off with a few minutes ago?"

I rubbed my hands over my arms to warm myself. "Yes. And something to do with the casino. The Magician is angry about the casino."

I held up my palms to respond to her what's-that-got-to-do-with-anything look.

"The casino?" Grady repeated. She rose and paced the room, her brows locked in concentration.

I pushed my wet bangs off my face. "Somehow there's a concentration of power near there."

"Like a vortex?"

I shrugged. "We don't know for sure, but Josh had a vision. He believes the Magician used the place for sacred healing, and now, for some reason, he can't."

Grady sat quietly and tapped the top of her desk

with both hands. I moved over to the chair nearby and waited without moving, almost without breathing, while she thought through these new facts.

Then she sprang up and headed for the door. "Come on," she called over her shoulder. "I want to show you something."

We headed down the hall at a full run, and she slammed through the door to the records room. "Where's the file on the casino's financials? It came in yesterday."

The clerk behind the desk looked confused and then frightened by Grady's intense expression.

"The Feds sent it a couple of days ago," Grady snapped.

The clerk pointed to a cardboard box on a shelf. Grady pushed through the half door and reached the shelf before the clerk had a chance to move, much less retrieve the file.

Grady carried the box, and we were back in her office in another moment. She locked the door. "We're safe here. I have new security. Manny insisted. Plus, my IT guy sweeps my office every morning."

Grady tore off the taped lid and dug into the file folders. "These came in just before Manny disappeared. I didn't…" she sucked in a quick breath. "I didn't have the guts to look at them yet." She handed me a file.

"You don't need to explain." I sat down to examine the first thick folder.

I wished my mother was here. She had years of snooping experience, and we could use her talent now. But bringing her in would take time, and she needed to stay with Gran and George at the ranch. Who knew where Patterson would strike next? We needed to

95

protect our family the best we could.

The casino officially belonged to the Yavapai tribe, and all moneys were overseen by a committee from the tribe...and the feds. It took several hours to cull through the last five years of the financial records, but we finally glommed onto some obscure money transfers the investigators had flagged.

"I'm not an accountant, but check this out. The auditors obviously thought the records were on the up-and-up, until this point." Grady pointed to a line marked in green felt tip pen in every quarterly report. The entry read "tribal artifacts."

"Artifacts?" I asked, rubbing my hands over my tired eyes.

Grady leaned back in her chair and stretched out her back. "I've been in that casino hundreds of times, mostly to arrest some drunk. I don't remember much in the way of ancient artifacts."

"Gran took me there once to hear a music group, but I didn't see anything besides a few made-in-China replicas. Maybe we could ask George."

Grady grunted. "Later. No time right now." She dug in the box and pulled out the next file, but a red casino chip contained in an evidence bag slipped from the folder and landed on her desk.

I stared at it for an instant, and then a massive wave of chills climbed up my arms and across my back. "Robb."

I picked up the bag and read the label. "The former sheriff." I waved the evidence bag in the air.

By this point even my toes had goose bumps. I had to take a couple of deep breaths before I could explain. Grady knew about her predecessor's legal troubles, but

I filled her in on the important events anyway.

"Sheriff Robb was after ancient artifacts from the tribe," I told her. "He was part of a conspiracy, and had been blackmailed into stealing artifacts."

"Oh, shit." Grady looked up from reading another file. "They weren't just stealing artifacts. They were stealing grave goods. Says here in the auditor's final report the firm believed someone was hoarding those artifacts, because none of the pieces could ever be tracked down. None of them were ever seen again, even on the black market."

A massive chill froze my heart. "Patterson."

****

I reached the top of the hill and stopped to look out over the desert valley. No highway hummed in the distance, no small town crept up the rocky hillsides. We were in a different time, the Magician's time.

Manny stood next to the Magician. He turned to me as I reached them and stared at me with sad eyes. I was breathing hard from the climb, and he took the spear from my hand so I could bend over and catch my breath.

"How's Grady?" he asked after I had a minute to recover.

I shook my head. "What do you think?"

He turned away and stared down the other side of the hill at the glowing fire burning below us.

My throat was jammed up with the words I wanted to say, but couldn't.

"It was my choice," Manny explained. "I could see where Patterson was leading us, what he would do if we couldn't—"

"Couldn't what? Stop him? Kill him?" I shouted.

He crossed his arms and spread his legs in a stubborn, I-know-what-I'm-doing stance. "I did what I did for everyone I love. I didn't want to, believe me. But the Magician showed me the future, and what Patterson is capable of doing—the power he has amassed. We have to stop him. This is the only way."

A cold rush of fear flowed over me. I swallowed nonexistent spit and moved up beside him. "What do you mean, we have to stop him. That's what WE have been trying to do all along." I reached out to touch his shoulder and pulled back in surprise.

My fingers stung with the icy cold of death. I looked up at him, and he dropped his chin.

Shit. Manny was a ghost.

I took a step back and started to run, but he was too fast for me. And he had the spear.

CHAPTER 13

Josh never came back.

Grady and I waited until late in the night. Around two, she sent out a team of deputies to search for him. I begged to go, but she wouldn't let me help.

The search party roamed into the hills, even though I was pretty sure I knew where Josh had been headed with the Magician.

Frustrated, worried, terrified, I sat on the steps of the sheriff's department until almost dawn.

Grady came out and tried to talk me into sleeping. "Just a couple of hours."

Yeah, right. I couldn't, of course, even after she had a deputy make up a bed for me and she practically dragged me into a spare room at the back.

Too tired to argue, I stared at the dark ceiling and listened to my heart thump in my chest. It was broken, and I knew it. The words hadn't been formed yet, the tears hadn't come, but as I lay there in the dark, I knew I was alone.

The search team returned by midmorning. Even though the cops never found his body, the coroner declared the crime scene at the top of the mountain proof of foul play. The broken spear covered with Josh's blood was evidence of his probable death.

Although hopeful search teams worked throughout the weekend, by the following Tuesday, the tribe scheduled a memorial for Josh.

****

Somehow, June arrived. The heat had been fierce all week, but I sat on the couch and wrapped the soft blue blanket around my shoulders. I couldn't get warm, even standing outside in the blazing sunshine.

Mom was wonderful, and Gran an absolute dear. They tiptoed around our apartment, and let me mourn in peace. Gran tried a time or two to get me to eat, but food, even chocolate cheesecake, tasted like mud.

My stomach revolted if I swallowed anything but cool water. I guess my body knew I only needed water for tears. I certainly cried enough.

George showed up Thursday afternoon, and Mom asked me if I wanted to see him. I shook my head and buried my face in a pillow.

She knelt beside me and rubbed my arm. "It might help to talk to him, Forrest. George has lost someone he dearly loves, too."

I turned to look into her calm, sad eyes. "How did you ever get through it? How did you keep going after Dad was …gone?" I choked out the word.

She sat beside me and took my hands in her strong fingers. "This loss will always be a part of you."

I moaned. How would I survive the week, much less a lifetime, if this was how I would always feel? Cold, and dead, and angry. "I can't think. I can't move. I can hardly breathe."

She squeezed my hands until I looked up at her. "Eventually the loss will settle into a place where you can deal with it more easily. The pain will recede from your immediate thoughts, your immediate feelings. In time you will even smile again."

"When?"

She stroked her cool hand over my cheek. "When you can think of others."

I sucked in some air and wiped my tears off my chin with the back of my hand. "Is George still here?"

"He's waiting for you at the overlook."

****

The sun beat down on my shoulders, and the heat took my breath away, but the hot wind dried my tears while I shuffled down the road to the rock wall by the lookout.

An old man sat on the bench nearby. I hardly recognized him until I looked into his eyes. George had lost weight in the week since Josh left. The lines around his eyes drooped with folds of grief, but he held out a hand, and I took hold.

George had taken Josh in as a poor orphan boy. He'd raised him to manhood, inspired him, loved him, and then lost him. I ached for him.

I folded my arms around his thin shoulders and held on to him. After a while, we sat shoulder to shoulder and watched wisps of clouds shadow the desert below.

He cleared his throat. "Norah's coming for the memorial." He still didn't look at me. "The track team's coming, and all the teachers will be there."

I drew circles with my finger against the hot rocks on the wall and chewed my lip for a moment. "I don't know, George. I'm not ready. I don't think I can face other people yet."

"He'd want you there."

My throat closed to more words, and I rested my head in my hands.

"Tomorrow. Newspaper rock. Sunset."

I nodded and walked home through the blistering heat. I would be there for George.

****

Having something to think about got me through the night. By morning, I had a plan.

I grabbed my keys before Mom was awake, left her a note, and drove to Verde in the fresh morning air. I remembered the first time I drove Josh up this hill. I almost chuckled at how tightly he gripped the chicken bar.

In a moment of pure insanity, I stomped the gas pedal and dared Tilley to take me over the side of the cliff.

Despite my moment of craziness, she stubbornly stayed on the road.

My heart refused to stop, my lungs still processed air. I clenched the steering wheel and ground my teeth so hard my jaw ached.

Maybe I did want to live. Maybe I did want to have a purpose, even if I never held Josh in my arms again.

I slowed Tilley to twenty above the speed limit and continued down the hill. I had a bucketload to do before sunset.

The gate to Manny's ranch stood open, but no cars were parked in front of his house. I stopped for a moment and studied the front porch, remembering the laughter I heard. Was that only days ago?

I drove the rest of the way to the barn and slowly opened the side door. Trouble called to me from his roost. I check his food and water bowls. Somebody had remembered to feed the poor orphan. Probably Grady, if I had to guess.

I hunted for the leather glove and slipped it on my hand. I closed my eyes to stop the tears. *Don't think about it, girl. Just do what needs to get done.*

I called to the bird and held up a chunk of dried meat. Trouble screeched a few times from the rafters. Was he lonely too? He beat his strong wings and gracefully flew down to land on the half wall next to me.

"Hello, darling," I cooed to him and stroked his strong chest with my other hand. I handed him the food, and he took it, swallowing quickly and looking for more.

I held up another bite, and placed my gloved hand beside his feet. He latched his strong talons onto my arm. My arm could barely support the almost full-grown eagle. He must weigh forty pounds, and his wingspan stretched at least five feet. Carefully, I walked him across the barn to his low roost of branches.

Trouble allowed me to stroke his back, and I spoke to him in low, comforting tones. He beat his wings a few times, and studied me closely. In the dim light of the barn, I looked into his eyes, and my breath caught.

Amber eyes. My heart bumped hard in my chest, and my throat seized up. Why had I never noticed before? No wonder the bond between Josh and this bird was so strong.

The bird watched me curiously as a tear dripped off my chin. I didn't want to scare him by sobbing out loud, so I bit my lip until it stung. I put the small leather hood over his head and attached the leather thongs to his strong legs.

The full-grown eagle hardly fit in his carrying crate

anymore, but after a struggle and a few choice words, I convinced him to go inside.

Standing outside the barn, I checked the time by the height of the sun against the western mountains, the way Josh taught me. I had about an hour to make Newspaper rock. Trouble waited impatiently on the front porch while I changed my clothes in my old room in Manny's cabin. I brushed my hair and washed my tear-stained, dusty face. I didn't know how I would get through the next few hours, but I didn't have a choice.

I would go to the memorial, but not for myself. I had to go for George, for my mother and Gran. For Grady, who had lost her Manny. But most of all I had to be there, for Josh. I squared my shoulders and walked out the door, letting the screen door bang behind me.

My new wingman and I reached the ranch gates near Newspaper Rock as the first of the red clouds settled over the western skyline. The heat was oppressive, way over a hundred degrees. I dug in the back for a bottle of water and downed the warm liquid in a couple of long gulps.

I recognized a few of the cars in the dusty parking lot, which was more crowded than I'd ever seen it. Some people I knew, but others I hardly recognized. Everyone trudged slowly along the dusty road toward the ancient monument. I waved to Zalo, but he didn't approach me.

Newspaper Rock, a huge stone covered in petroglyphs, was sacred to the Yavapai. Once again the area was open to respectful visitors. The tribe had pulled together enough money to purchase the land when it came up for sale after Patterson disappeared.

I removed Trouble's head covering and thongs

while keeping him inside the cage. After I lifted the cage out of Tilley, I headed toward the rock. The crowd parted as I made my way to the front. George stood nearby, speaking quietly to a few of the elders.

My mom and Gran moved to my side. Mom smiled and took my free hand. Gran gave me a peck on the cheek. She was dressed in red, the mourning color for the Yavapai. Grady smiled at me from across the crowd.

I don't know if anyone noticed Trouble. The bird didn't make so much as peep in his cage. During the short ceremony given by one of the chiefs in Yavapai, I only understood a few words. The word for love caught in my throat, and Mom put her arm around me to keep me steady. I ducked my head to keep my tears to myself.

Coach got up and said a few words. Most of the guys on the team were sniffling by this point. The back of my throat hurt so much I almost ran back to Tilley. I couldn't take much more, but Gran stood next to me, her arm around my waist, and I managed to dig up one more shred of courage.

A few of the girls on the track team, and some from our class, placed wildflowers on the rock.

George turned to me, his eyes red and blurry, his mouth bracketed by deep grooves of heartache. "Do you want to say anything, Forrest? You were his closest friend. He loved you."

I dashed back my tears and squared my shoulders. I bent, lifted Trouble out of his cage, and marched forward. The eagle didn't struggle as I held him close, his wings folded, his gaze focused on me. As the crowd hushed, the wind whistled through the palo verde trees nearby.

"This is Josh's friend," I held up the bird, both hands carefully wrapped around his wings. "His name is Trouble." I said with almost a laugh. The bird waited, warm and heavy in my hands. As if he knew, as if he knew...

"He's pretty cool, and Josh loved him." A murmur rippled through the group, but I kept going. "Josh trained him, as is the custom of the Yavapai tribe, but deep in his soul, it hurt Josh to know the bird would never be free."

Trouble gave a long, piercing screech.

I licked my dry lips. "So, buddy, now you can be free. Josh would have wanted it this way."

I tossed the bird into the air, and the breeze caught under the eagle's wide wings. He beat them against the wind and rose above us. He circled twice, moving higher and higher, and with one joyful call, flew north out of sight.

"Goodbye," I whispered.

CHAPTER 14

Mom drove me home. I was in no shape to get behind the wheel, so Grady had one of the deputies deliver Tilley. I barely managed to climb the stairs before my strength gave out.

Gran put me to bed like I was three, and Mom made me drink some honeyed tea. I think she spiked it, because it was the first time I'd slept in days. When I woke up the next morning, the clock read ten.

I shuffled out into the living room, wondering what I would do with the rest of my life. There didn't seem to be anything left I cared about. Nothing important I wanted to do.

I stared at the acceptance letter from the U taped to our little fridge and dragged in a deep breath. Three weeks ago, I'd been dancing around the kitchen. A scholarship, a chance to be a cop had seemed like a dream come true.

Now I didn't give a shit.

"Forrest? There's someone here to see you," my mom called up the stairs.

I heard footsteps and grimaced. I did not feel like talking to anyone, much less a stranger.

The woman, tall and beautiful, with piercing dark eyes and native skin, smiled openly. She mounted the last few steps and moved closer. "Hello, Forrest. It's good to finally meet you. Josh told me so much about you."

I cringed at the mention of his name and stared at her without recognition.

She looked around the room. "Your mom and Gran have done a lovely job with this room. I saw it before—" She cleared her throat. "When it wasn't so pretty."

I flopped on the couch, grabbed a pillow and hugged it to my chest.

"Maybe I should introduce myself."

I'd already rummaged around in Norah's thoughts until I figured out who she was. "You're Norah. Josh's mentor."

"Why, yes." She seemed surprised for a moment, and then tipped her head to the side as if to study me.

"You helped Josh when he was younger, after his mother died. After his creepy uncle stole him."

She took a step closer and brushed one long hank of black hair back from her face. A few streaks of silver glinted in the light.

"You taught him how to shield himself," I continued. "Trained him so he wouldn't go bonkers every time he touched something and knew creepy stuff about it."

I stood and walked around her slowly. "You knew the Magician."

"Did Josh tell you all that?" Norah asked patiently, her face still calm and her shoulders relaxed.

I shrugged one shoulder. "Most of it. But it's right here." I pointed my index finger at her forehead and gave it a little shove.

"What else can you do? What other gifts do you have?" Norah kept her gaze steady and her voice low, like she was trying to hypnotize me or something.

I flopped back on the couch. "I see ghosts now, too."

Norah seemed to think for a moment, then settled on the chair opposite me. She smoothed her skirt with one hand and then glanced up. She'd blocked my readings by this point. She was strong and talented, but there was something more. Something Josh had never spoken about. I guess I would just have to wait for her tell me.

"I'm here to help you, Forrest. I'm here to help Josh."

I gave a derisive snort and folded my legs under me. "Little late for that."

"No. It's not too late, but I'll need your patience if we're going to succeed. It's been a while since I've had these visions, these awful feelings, and I will have to move slowly in order to get it right. Are you willing to help me?"

I squinted at her for a long moment, and she let me see enough to know she wasn't goofing with me. She was being totally truthful, but there was fear at the back of her mind. Shivers rolled over my arms and legs like the cold ocean waves of the Pacific near my old home in California.

"That was a very brave thing you did at the service."

"You were there?"

She gave me a slow nod. "Freeing the bird meant a lot to you."

I stared out the window and fought back the tears brimming my eyes.

She moved over next to me and took my hand. "It meant a lot to Josh, too."

"What did you mean, you have visions?"

Norah gave me a huge smile. "I'm so glad you're open to these experiences, Forrest. I've had people who wanted to throw me out of their houses, when I talked to them about going back in time."

I guess my mouth must have hung open for a moment. I pushed my jaw back up with my thumb. "What'd you say?"

"Let me start from the beginning, but first there is something I need you to do." She walked to the stairs and called to my mom. "She's ready."

"Ready for what?"

"To eat. To get strong again."

"I'm not hungry."

"I know. It was a terrible loss for everyone. I understand." She crossed her arms and studied me. "But if I'm going to help you...and you're going to help Josh, you need to be at your best."

Mom appeared at the top of the stairs and ducked into the kitchen. She came out with a large bowl of soup and crackers and set it on the table.

Hope stirred in my soul, and suddenly food smelled good again. My stomach rumbled. I walked over, sat, and finished off the bowl.

"She'll need more," Norah called into the kitchen.

After two more bowls and some chocolate chip cookies, I felt a lot better, boosted by the lovely sugar buzz racing through my bloodstream.

"Tell me now," I said.

"Get cleaned up first. Take a long, hot shower, and let your mind wander away from the pain."

I followed Norah's orders, and only came out when the water ran cold. Mom had laid a soft cotton dress on my bed, and I slipped it over my head. Then I combed my hair back from my face. My eyes were still bloodshot, but I could see I looked calmer, more together, more *me*, than I had in days.

I walked back into the living room. Norah had a cup of tea on her lap and chuckled at something Gran had just told her.

"So you've only just discovered this talent?" Norah took another sip.

Gran nodded, looking totally proud of herself. "The gene pool finally pulled together. I guess everyone has their time." She tucked a stray curl back into her bright purple scarf and blushed. "I must admit, the feeling is very satisfying. Being able to help people has given me a real sense of purpose."

When Gran saw me, she patted the seat beside her. "Norah knew Josh when he was a little boy."

I smiled into my grandmother's softly lined face. "Yes, he told me." I glanced around the room. "Where's Mom?"

Norah set down her cup. "I asked her to go find George and bring him here. She called that friend of yours, the police officer..."

"Grady?"

"We need everyone who is a part of the story to be together in one room," Norah explained. "I need to understand the details."

"What for?'

"So I can send you back in time."

CHAPTER 15

Norah glanced around the living room at our small group. In a way, I felt like we were gathered to prepare for battle. Like each of us—George, Grady, my mom and Gran—every one of us would need our skills and our courage if we were to help Josh.

I swallowed the sticky lump in my throat and held my mother's hand. These people were my family. They all wanted to help me, to help Josh, and they would risk their own safety to do what they could.

With her face set in solemn lines, Norah stood and began her speech. "I met Josh when he was only twelve, and he was living in a children's shelter. He'd just lost his mother, although the police didn't know yet she had been murdered."

Even with a soft smile of remembrance on her face, her voice carried heavy tones of sadness. She ushered me into her mind, and I saw the small, frightened boy she rescued. I gasped when I saw this sad, fearful version of my Josh.

George drew a hand down his braid, a sign he was nervous, but then added. "I met him soon after that, although he didn't come to live with me until he finished his training with you."

I glanced over a Norah. "You helped him develop his shields?"

"Yes. I think he'd already begun the process

112

himself out of pure self- preservation. He was a quick study." Norah looked up at the group. "Did he use his ability to read objects much in the past few years?"

I shook my head. "After we started seeing each other, he told me about his gift. He demonstrated it once or twice, but didn't like to do it often. I only asked him to read something once, and that was a disaster."

"But he did learn from the Magician's tools," George said. "He knew the history of each of those artifacts, plus what the Magician showed him in visions."

Norah focused on George. "And besides the encounters with the Magician, what was his focus?"

"Josh just wanted to be a normal kid. He wanted to run track, go to college," George choked on the word, but drew in a noisy breath and continued. "He studied hard. He wanted to be a doctor."

"The Magician wanted him to be a doctor," I corrected George. "But Josh had totally bought into the idea. He worked very hard to earn a scholarship."

Norah studied me closely. "Why do you think he decided on medicine as a career?"

I turned away and hunched my shoulders to keep the tears from taking over again. "The Magician showed him a healing vision." The tears came anyway. "M-Manny was there, too."

Grady hitched in a short breath and turned to face the wall. She hadn't said two words during the whole meeting, but she'd been listening so carefully. She was pretending to be strong.

"Josh didn't tell you, Grady, because he didn't know yet."

Grady put up one hand. "I get it."

"The spear appeared in the last vision," I continued. "A new tool. One Josh had never seen before. Josh told me there were eagle feathers on the spear in the vision, but none remained when it came to him in our world."

I stared out the window. "And then there was Trouble."

"The eagle?" Norah asked.

I nodded. Unable to sit still, I rose and paced the room, talking so fast my mouth could hardly keep up with the words. "He really, really didn't want to sacrifice Trouble. I knew that from the first moment he brought the bird home. He never said as much, but I knew the truth."

I searched the faces of my friends. "I'd promised not to read him, and I always kept that promise, but sometimes his thoughts were just there." I dropped my eyes to the floor. "Sometimes we were so close, I just knew."

"He told me the same thing. He wanted to find another way," George added. "It weighed on his heart, because he loved the bird."

"When was the last time he saw the Magician? Or had a vision?" Norah asked.

"The night after Manny disappeared, the Magician called him. We were out at the ranch, and Josh went to the salt mines. The Magician showed him another vision and gave him the spear." I swallowed the searing lump in my throat. "The next day, we took some tail feathers from Trouble, and Josh attached them so it looked the same as in the vision."

I stared out the window for a moment. "Josh wouldn't let me follow him. The Magician...the

Magician was standing on the hill, waiting for Josh. I could see him, and Josh ran to him."

I glanced at Norah. "I don't think what happened was supposed to happen. Josh wasn't afraid."

"Why should he have been afraid?" George interrupted. "The Magician never harmed him before."

I rubbed my eyes and sank back on the couch. "I don't think the Magician did harm him."

Norah rose and circled around the others to sit next to me. She put an arm around my shoulders and rubbed my arms gently.

Tears fell almost without my knowing, and I leaned into her for comfort. "Can you help him?"

Norah took my face in her hands and pulled my chin level with hers, her gaze focused. "Yes. But it won't be easy, and there will be sacrifice."

I brushed back my tears and sucked in a clean breath. "I'll do anything."

"Forrest." Mom moved over beside me. "This could be difficult. You shouldn't make promises you might not be able to keep."

"I don't care." Hysteria closed in. My blood pounded in my brain, and my voice rose. "I don't care what it takes. I can't let Josh just die without doing… something."

Norah squeezed my hand and turned to face my mom. "I promise you, no physical harm will come to Forrest, but her journey will require immense courage."

Gran stood and walked purposefully toward the deck of Tarot cards she still kept near the fireplace. She spread them over the surface of the small mantel and drew one from the middle, then waved it for all of us to see. "We never finished the reading."

She drew a card and handed it to me, saying, "This card represents the views of others or external influences."

I glanced at Norah.

The card read, *Queen of Cups*. A beautiful woman sat on a throne, holding a golden chalice. She was surrounded by a flowing river.

"A fair woman will do a service. She has a gift of vision and wisdom. See?" Gran asked. "The cup has winged angels."

"Is this Norah?"

Gran gave a quick shrug. "Maybe. Or maybe this is you."

Cold chills raced over me, but the pain of loss had subsided, and hope surged through me. I could help Josh. I turned to Mom. "What about Patterson?"

A tweak of a smile flashed across my mother's face, but then the sadness in her expression returned. "Whatever Josh did, he defeated Patterson, at least for now. The man and his power are gone. I can feel it."

CHAPTER 16

I had two weeks to prepare.

Norah wrote out a page-long set of instructions. Jeez, what a drill sergeant.

Eat this, don't eat that. Sleep long hours. Run. It was like I was training for a big fight. I could almost hear *Rocky* music playing as I ran the steps to the park ten times every day. But in a week, I was strong. In two, I was awesome.

After the last flight of stairs on Saturday morning, I stood and looked out over the valley. I was breathing hard, but not gasping like a week ago. And I'd put on three pounds, in all the right places. My running shorts didn't fall off my hips anymore.

I bit down on my lip and shoved back the threatening tears. No more crying. No more heartbreak. Even if I couldn't glue my heart back together, at least I could damn well stop feeling sorry for myself. Grief was different from self-pity. I knew that now.

I crossed the street to Angel's Cloud and waved to Gran behind the counter. She'd just finished taking a picture of some tourist's aura with her new digital camera. I rolled my eyes and headed up the stairs.

I ducked into my room and tossed my sweaty clothes in a pile on the floor. Mom had hung my graduation gown on the front of the closet door. Silky red. Next to the gown, a small gold tassel dangled from the corny square hat. I let the strands flow through my fingers. Two more days.

In two more days, I would walk in a line without Josh, onto a stage without Josh. Out into a new life, without Josh.

A tap sounded on my open door, and Norah waved a quick hello.

"Hey," I said, slipping into a clean cotton tee.

"Yours is blue mostly."

"My what is mostly blue?"

"I noticed how you reacted to the aura photograph your Gran was taking."

"I'm sorry. I didn't see you when I came in."

"That's okay." Norah studied the space around me, as if she was looking at something a foot beyond the edge of my body.

"There's lots of green, too. That color stands for change."

"You can see auras?"

"Sometimes. Come out to the living room when you're ready." She closed the door softly behind her, and I was alone.

Really alone.

I swallowed the bitterness lurking at the back of my throat and rubbed my palms together to warm myself. Was I ready?

At least I could listen with an open mind.

****

Norah sat on our lumpy old couch across from the window. She'd tied her dark hair back in a messy knot and watched me carefully as I joined her. "You're in much better spirits than when I last saw you. You look stronger."

"I can function," I said with a shrug. "I don't feel much of anything right now."

"That's often the case with grief. At least I've come to help quickly. I knew a woman once who lived with this kind of mistake for almost seven years."

"A person she cared for had died?"

"Yes, someone she thought she loved." Norah rolled her shoulders, just as I had. Maybe she needed to relax, too. I tried to catch of glimpse of her thoughts, but she was totally walled off.

"Did you succeed with her?" I couldn't believe we were having this conversation. I guess if you've lived with weirdness most of your life, a little more weirdness kinda feels natural.

"Difficult? Yes. But we saved both men."

"What was the tough part?"

"Convincing her in the first place." Norah shook her head. "Lord, what a stubborn woman. I swear she considered having me committed."

"It is a bit..." I searched for a word that wasn't totally insulting and couldn't come up with one.

"Crazy?

"Well, yeah."

"Figuring out the right moment was the most difficult part. Sometimes it can be painful, and takes a few tries."

I tipped my head, caught up in the conversation and the natural way she spoke of such wacko ideas. "The right moment for what?"

"The moment to change time." Norah's steady, you-have-to-believe-me gaze caught me off guard even more than the crazy ideas that she was going on about.

"That's a new one."

"Yes. It's been a number of years since I've tried to alter time. My gifts changed dramatically when I met my husband, and I'm rarely called anymore."

"So you're married? Kids?"

"Two. Plus my niece I adopted earlier, before I met Jackson." Her smile warmed, and her eyes softened. For a second, she let me see her family.

"They're nice." I let out a longer sigh than I meant to. "You all look so happy together."

"It's understandable you're sad now, Forrest. You've lost a special person, someone who meant so much to you. To all of us."

"But we're going to get him back, right?"

Her smile remained, but her eyes lost the loving warmth of a few moments ago.

"Forrest, I can save Josh, but the life you have lived over the past couple of years will be forever changed."

I frowned, not understanding, and my stomach gave a sick tumble. "You promised. You promised you could save him." The painful plea flowed from somewhere deep in my soul. "Then we'll be together, and we'll go to college. Someday we'll get married, because we"—my breath caught— "we love each other."

Norah took my cold, trembling hands in hers. "Forrest, listen to me."

"You promised." The last word turned into a wail.

"Here is what I know." She squeezed my hands tighter and caught my gaze with hers. "You and Josh were not meant to meet."

"But I love him."

"I know. But that will have to change."

I shook my head ferociously, but Norah hung on to me even when I tried to get up and run.

She took hold of my shoulders and gave me a quick shake. "Do you want Josh to live?"

"Of course," I whispered.

"Then you have to do as I say. All of this," she moved her hand through the air over her head. "All of this is wrong. You were never meant to meet. Never meant to be together. Never meant to fall in love."

"But I saved him before, when Patterson tried to kill him."

"I know. Your mom told me the story. I know about everything. But you and Josh were too young to deal with what's happening. Too young to fight Patterson. And Josh was too young to die."

She let go of my hand, and I scrambled to the window facing the street. It took a few minutes for my breath to return, but after I calmed down, I turned to face her. Norah still sat in the same place, looking almost as distraught as I felt.

"The first time Josh came here, he had a vision. I remember the frightened look on his face."

"Yes, his Uncle Kenny hid him here when he was much younger. Jackson and I were searching for him. In fact," she rose, walked to the window, and pointed down into the busy street below. "I was standing right there, looking up into this window that very day, searching for him."

"He was cold and afraid."

"Kenny was a cruel man."

"I held on to Josh and helped him through the memory."

"You were a wonderful comfort to him. A true

friend. This is not your fault, Forrest. You didn't make any mistakes." Norah leaned on the window ledge and threw up her hands in frustration. "Sometimes mistakes happen through no one's fault. For many years, it was my calling to help undo those mistakes."

I tipped my head back and stared at the ceiling. "And now I have to undo this one."

****

Mom made tea for us and disappeared back downstairs with Gran. Nora and I sat at the table in the center of the room.

"Tell me about the first time you met," Norah took a sip and stirred in a bit more sugar.

I couldn't help smiling, thinking about Josh hiding behind that stupid bush by the river. I focused on the memory of his face. So young. So cute.

"The day started off pretty normal, but then everything went really freaky. I'd stayed late at school to finish a homework project, and decided to go for a short hike along the river before I drove back up to Jerome."

"Where was Josh?"

"In the canyon. Near this petroglyph of his cat."

"Like the one on the necklace?"

"You know about that, too?"

Norah must have caught the hint of surprise in my voice, and she chuckled. "Even before Josh worked with the Magician, I helped that old ghost, too. I've been to the gravesite on the cliff, and even spent a night in the salt mines."

I let out a long whistle, but then closed my eyes to remember our first meeting clearly. Somehow the horrible weight pressing on my chest lifted just a little, and I drew in a clean breath. "It was a glorious, sunny day. Warm but not hot. I'd walked up stream maybe a mile, and noticed him by the river, just sitting there, looking so sad. He must have heard me coming, because he hid in some bushes."

I rubbed my hands on my knees. "I wasn't going to put up with that, so I went over and started talking to him. I embarrassed him into coming out to talk to me. He said he didn't want to be a native guide if I was with a bunch of tourists." I fiddled with the hem of my dress. "A flimsy excuse, if you ask me. Of course, I'd noticed him at school, too. All the girls had a crush on him, but he seemed totally oblivious to all of them."

"But not to you."

I played with the hem of my dress some more, taking a moment to relive the romance of our meeting. "He was so sweet. He even claimed he liked Gran's whole grain cookies I shared with him, and they're totally awful. We only talked for maybe five minutes. I needed to head home, so I walked toward the trailhead, but after I saw the body, he must have heard my screams. He came running back. I was a total mess."

"I can imagine," Norah said.

"He helped me calm down, called the cops, and got me through the interview with Sheriff Rob. From that point on, we were…" I fiddled with my hair, twisting a strand around my finger. "We were together."

"Have you been intimate?"

My faced burned, and Norah took my silence for a yes.

"Just once, right before."

"Are you pregnant?"

"No, of course not. We were careful. We wanted to

go to school. We wanted to have a life together. We had plans." I said the last word and realized the futility of everything. I dropped my hands into my lap and sighed. "It's all gone, isn't it?"

Norah settled back, resting against the back of the chair. "If we do this, your life will change. There's no way for me to see where your path will lead once the change is complete. But I *am* certain Josh will live if you go through with this. He'll fulfill the destiny he was meant to have."

"But not with me."

"No."

"How do you know? Why isn't the person who needs to change stuff George or maybe…my mother?"

"Because when I look at you, and only you, your form is blurred. The green aura I spoke of earlier…that color, as much as anything, is the signal I receive every time. That's how I knew you needed help. I saw your green aura at the funeral, and I knew I had work to do."

I stared at the ceiling for a long moment. "Will I remember?"

Norah rubbed her shoulders with one hand. "Difficult to know. Some people do. Some people remember almost everything from both times. Some people go on with their lives and never experience a backward glance."

"I won't forget," I said, more to myself than to her.

She gave me a hopeful smile. "One woman did reconnect with the man she really loved. It could happen, or it could never happen. I have no more control over the future than you do."

I closed my eyes and rubbed my eyes with my palms. "I have to think."

****

I didn't sleep all night. I tried, but when I closed my eyes, Josh's face kept stirring through my thoughts. Josh's hands touched my face. Josh's lips kissed mine. I ached for him. I ached to sit beside him. To talk and laugh with him. To just *be* with him.

I must have dozed off about dawn. Mom knocked on my door at nine and brought me a cup of coffee. I sat in bed and drank the strong, black brew and hunted for my courage. I seemed to have misplaced it somewhere. I couldn't push my body out of bed for the longest time. Maybe I could just hide under the pillows and never come out again.

What would Josh think of Norah's plan? Would he want me to follow through and change our past? His past?

I fiddled with my hair for another moment and then sat straight up when the best idea ever burst into my brain.

My heart started to beat with a hopeful rhythm. I could talk to ghosts. Why not talk to him?

I was dressed in grubbies in less than a minute and sprinted for the door.

"Forrest?" my mother called as I grabbed my keys and rushed past her. I hadn't taken Tilley out in more than a week. Hopefully she'd start.

I slowed to call over my shoulder. "I'll be back in a couple of hours." And then I headed down the stairs.

The road from Jerome to Verde was a joy to drive. The cool breeze of morning tossed my hair. I ground Tilley's gears and revved her into a frenzy of quick turns. Don't ask me how I knew where to go. I just did. And I needed to be there ASAP. Josh was waiting.

I crawled into the dark tunnel and turned on all the lights I could find. The crystals sparkled, and for once I enjoyed the magic of the cavern. I sat down dead center in the cave and emptied a second water bottle before I composed myself.

Happily, I waited to be haunted.

CHAPTER 17

I'd never called a ghost before. What number should I dial? I hoped Josh was around, watching, so he'd know I was here. Problem was, I didn't sleep the night before, and in this quiet, peaceful place, with my heart relieved of the pain of separation, I had to fight to keep my eyes open. I leaned against the wall and let my eyes rest.

A cool breeze washed over my face, and then he was there. Even before I opened my eyes, I knew Josh was beside me. His warmth, his essence—I would know it anywhere. I kept my eyes shut tight, but reached out, and he took my hand, squeezing it lightly with his strong fingers.

Hi, Josh said, just like it was any day of the week.

"I've missed you," I whispered to my ghost.

Missed you too. He touched my face, drawing his hand down the side of my cheek in such a simple, loving gesture. Tears gathered in my eyes.

Don't cry, Forrest.

I finally had the courage to open my eyes and watched him for a long minute. "It's all I've done."

His lips pressed together in a brief, heartfelt frown, but then he kissed me.

"Show me," I whispered in his ear. "I need to understand. Please, Josh. What should I do next?"

His thoughts entwined with mine, and I ran with

him up a pine-covered hill. The Magician waited for us near the top. We followed him until we reached a ridge I'd never hiked before, and I looked out over the valley. The casino glowed in the distance. Its garish lights glared against the growing darkness of the desert.

"Is this where the Magician brought you before?"

Yes.

"What does he want?"

For the last of his tools to be returned to him.

"But you brought him the spear and even the eagle feathers. Wasn't that enough to stop Patterson?"

We didn't need to stop him. We needed to help him.

"How?"

We needed to help him move on.

Now I was more confused than ever. I had more questions, but Josh shook his head and tucked my hand under his arm. He hugged me to him, and I could feel his warmth, his breath, his heart against mine.

"Can I stay with you?"

You can't.

"It's too hard to be without you."

Norah will help. Listen to her.

"Should I go through with what she says? Should I undo time?"

He pointed out over the dark desert.

A small fire rose in the distance, and grew into a beacon. Shadows of people moved around it. Josh led me down the hill toward the gathering. The Magician, in full regalia, stood behind the flames. Manny stood to one side. Josh moved to the other.

From out of the darkness, Patterson limped forward.

I stepped back, and my heart rattled in my chest.

Did ghosts do battle?

Seemed likely. But instead of fighting, Josh helped Patterson take a seat by the glowing fire. They all turned to me, and seemed to be waiting for me to do something.

The Magician raised the spear, and I was returned to the crystal cave. Josh stood beside me, and I held on to him. When he stepped away, I reached for him, but he disappeared, and I dropped to my knees with a cry of pain.

"Love will survive."

Josh spoke the thought in my head, but I disagreed. I'd never been more alone.

****

Norah was waiting for me when I returned to Jerome. I was a mess, covered in salt dust, my face streaked with tears. But I was determined to move forward with her plan.

What else could I do? Josh would not come back to me any other way.

"Let's get to it," I said.

Norah insisted on nourishment first. Were all mothers like that?

And a shower. I did look a wreck. I hurried through both, barely rinsing the soap out of my hair. But soon I was fed, dressed, and ready.

When Norah asked Mom and Gran to leave, they objected. Only after I insisted I was fine did they grudgingly agree. After telling me they'd be waiting at Rocky's for our call, Mom helped Gran down the steps, and they left. I waved to them as they closed the door and hurried over to the Rocky's outdoor seating area.

Norah had positioned herself on the floor.

Excitement rippled through me with hot and cold shivers as I joined her there. "What next?"

"We need to decide on a time to change."

I screwed my eyes up, more confused than ever. "Should I leave Jerome? Never go to school here?"

Norah considered my questions for a long moment, but shook her head. "No. You need to be in Jerome. There are people here you must know. This is where you and your family belong."

"So it's only knowing Josh that needs to change?"

"Knowing him then," she elaborated, "when you were both so young."

"Well then, the river was our first real meeting."

Norah closed her dark eyes, sat very still for a moment, and then nodded. "That feels right." She took a small leather pouch from her side and crumpled some dried herbs into an old bowl. The smell of sage and something sweet struck my nose.

"Try to relax," Norah said in a soothing, sing-song voice.

"Riiiight." I had to snicker, but then I rolled my shoulders and concentrated on letting my muscles and mind relax.

She reached over and took a drum into her lap. Tapping with her fingers on the old hide, she began a slow, monotonous pattern of beats.

The rhythm cascaded through me, and I closed my eyes. Another ripple of excitement cascaded over me, and suddenly my heart felt lighter, and I smiled to myself. I would see Josh again.

****

I stripped off my shoes and socks and dunked my feet in the cool river. The afternoon was still warm, although with the sun setting in an hour, the worst of the heat had passed.

Gran promised the summer swelter would soon break, and I would learn to like the desert a little more. Right now it was a hot, miserable place, with strange plants and creepy-crawly snakes and bugs I didn't want to think about it too much.

Dribbling cool water over my legs, I glanced up at the heat-bleached sky, wishing we had never been forced to move to Arizona, but I guess ghost towns were few and far between in Northern California. Gran had it in her head she could become a fortune teller. I twisted my mouth and spat out a quick laugh. Not likely.

I dried my toes with my socks and glanced upstream. Ahead, next to the river, someone told me there were some way old, cool drawings carved into the sides of the canyon walls. I got up and dusted off the back of my shorts and legs, deciding to hike deeper into the canyon and check out the animals and designs people scratched into the walls. It was spooky to think about people living here so many years ago.

A couple of hundred yards upstream, I hopped over another boulder and looked up just in time to see movement out of the corner of my eye. My heart jumped into my throat for a second, but it was only a teenage native boy in jeans and an old T-shirt.

He'd been sitting on the sand by the river, but now moved behind a large green tree to try to hide himself, crouching down behind the bush.

How rude.

Of course, I knew who he was. I'd seen him at school a few times. In a school the size of ours, it was hard not to know everyone in a matter of days.

I fisted my hands on my hips and gave a quick snort. I could take a hint. If Josh Kwail didn't feel like socializing, who was I to stop and be friendly?

Besides, Gran wanted me home before dark. I stopped to catch my breath, then turned back toward my car. I'd check out the petroglyphs another day, when the canyon was a little less crowded.

CHAPTER 18

12 years later.
I folded my white coat and stuffed the weekend bag in the passenger seat. George was waiting for me in Camp Verde, and I wanted to be home before dark. I glanced back at the hospital where I'd spent most of the last nine years working and studying. Now, finally, the letters MD followed my name.

Dr. Josh Kwail, MD. I grinned to myself. It had a nice ring to it.

I liked the feel of the car keys in my pocket, so I took them out once more and stared at the fob to my new truck. After I drew my hand over the slick red paint of the hood and slid into the cushy driver's seat, I pushed the button labeled Start.

I had to listen carefully to hear the purr of the engine, but a subtle rumble transmitted through the steering wheel. I set the gear to drive and was on my way home.

Over the past eight—no, almost nine—years, I drove from the University in Tucson to Verde often enough in my fifteen-year-old Chevy. I made it home for most of the holidays with George, but the demands of medical school, then an internship, and finally a residency in internal medicine, had kept me away from the Verde Valley for longer and longer periods every year.

Now I was returning to build my practice in our small town, and to care for the people of our tribe.

Anxious to be home, I only stopped in Phoenix for gas and a couple of tacos before heading north the last hundred miles to Camp Verde. It was almost twilight before I pulled my new wheels out of the last rest stop onto the highway. Twenty miles to home.

Maybe George would make chili for dinner. My mouth watered at the thought, and I smiled through the sudden glare on my windshield. Accelerating up over the rise, I must have been doing eighty.

That's when I spied the cop on the side of the road. Dammit. Nailed by radar. I saw the red and blue squad car lights flash, and then the officer pulled up next to me and waved me over rather than blasting me with a siren.

"Damn," I said again under my breath. After driving a junker for years, I finally had a car that could do the speed limit. My luck I'd get jammed up with a ticket before I even made it home for dinner.

Disgusted with myself, I signaled and parked on the side of the road and waited for the officer to make his…no, wait, *her* way to the passenger side of the truck. I rolled down the window and smiled.

"Sorry, officer." I tried to sound contrite. "I guess I didn't realize how fast this little truck would go." I handed over my license and hot-off-the-presses registration before I was even asked. No point in lying. I'd been nabbed fair and square.

That's when I took another look at the officer as she straightened and examined my papers. When she leaned in again, she looked at me carefully.

My breath caught in my throat as I met her blue-green eyes and experienced a strange sort of deep recognition. "Have we met?"

She smiled. A beautiful, warm smile that brightened her whole face. "Josh?"

"Yeah."

And that's when she said, "Welcome home, Dr. Kwail."

Epilogue

The small crowd gathered around us cheered at the end of my story. I raised my champagne glass and scanned out over the roomful of familiar faces.

Friends like Manny and Grady, now holding their two-year-old, smiled back at me. George, his braids now totally silver, held up his glass and clinked it with Forrest's mom and Gran. Even Zalo took the weekend off from law school at ASU to join us for the ceremony.

I turned to look at Forrest. My bride stood beside me, and I squeezed her hand in mine. She still took my breath away every time I saw her, and I would remember this moment as long as I lived. Forrest smiled back at me, her blue-green waterfall eyes alight with love. The love of my life, the woman who saved me, stood beside me. Somehow, we both remembered the day we first met by the river, and first met yet again on the highway outside of town. Norah shrugged when we asked her to explain.

We turned together and gazed out over the construction site of the new hospital. In the last of the evening light, lit by the full moon rising in the east, I could see the casino sign lying flat in the parking lot, while the new Yavapai Tribal Hospital sign glowed softly with blue light.

I pointed to the sky, and Forrest squinted as we followed two large birds circling above us. Trouble gave a piercing cry and disappeared over the horizon with his mate.

It had taken several years to convince the Tribal Council that our new facility had to be placed where the defunct casino once stood. Now the hotel was being converted to patient rooms. The old gambling halls would house surgery, emergency, and state-of-the-art treatment and diagnostic facilities. The refitting was almost complete, thanks to the bequest of an anonymous donor.

In a special glass cabinet near the entry, the Magician's tools were on display. The cat necklace, my first gift from the Magician, held a place of honor. On either side, the seed basket and water bowl were displayed. Behind them, the spear decorated with three eagle feathers stood in a special holder.

Only the courting flute was missing. I had tucked that in the pocket of my tux and would return it after our honeymoon.

Acknowledgements.

Of course, a huge thank-you goes to my family, who put up with me while I was writing and revising this book. A special hug goes to my Dear Hubby, Dave, my major supporter, fan and technical support.

Thank you to the Armadillos, my critique group, and all the other friends and neighbors who read and sometimes re-read the manuscript, especially my great friends, Patti and Kathy.

To the owners of the Connor Hotel (yes, it's a real place) and the Haunted Hamburger. I love the settings of Jerome and the Verde Valley. Forgive me for taking license with these locations. I have purposefully obscured the location of several historical sites to protect them.

I also have deliberately misguided the reader regarding the location of the petroglyph of the saber-toothed cat, and the possible location of the Magician's grave.

And yes, there was a Magician, buried centuries ago in a different canyon. I had fun bringing him back to life.

A word about the author...

Along with teaching, Joy began her writing career by publishing children's historical fiction. She later found writing romantic suspense fulfilled her need for travel and romance. She lives with her husband and two dogs near Silicon Valley and the mythical town of Sereno. http://www.ejbrighton.com

Thank you for purchasing
this publication of The Wild Rose Press, Inc.

For questions or more information
contact us at
info@thewildrosepress.com.

The Wild Rose Press, Inc.
www.thewildrosepress.com